searching for risk

Tonya Burrows

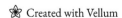

part one
ignite

I am only a spark: Make me a fire.

Amado Nervo

episode 1: what happened to darcy?

Hey there, Truth Seekers! Welcome to Cold Truth, the podcast that's all about uncovering the mysteries of cold cases. I'm your host, Alexis Summers, and I'm thrilled to be taking you on a journey into the baffling case of Darcy Cantrell - a teenage girl who vanished without a trace.

Now, I know true crime can be a bit heavy, but don't worry - I'm here to guide you through the twists and turns of this intriguing case, and I'll try to keep things as light as possible.

So, pop in your earbuds and get ready to join me each week as we unravel the chilling truth behind Darcy's disappearance.

Darcy Cantrell never expected to live a long life. She never expected to be famous, either. Not with where and who she came from. Her mom, Sissy, had struggled with addiction her whole life and died of a heroin overdose when Darcy was only nine. Her dad, Franklin, was an abusive asshole when he was home—which, thankfully, as a commercial fisherman, wasn't often. She was mainly left to fend for herself, and she preferred it that way.

I know we say this next thing a lot in true crime—so

much, it's become a cliche—but in this case, there's no other word to describe Darcy. She was stunning and she could light up a room—when she wanted to. At eighteen, she wore her dark hair in a shaggy, shoulder-length bob and had piercing gray eyes that changed color with her mood. She was tall and thin and if she'd been born into another family, she might have gone on to be a model or an actress, capitalizing on her beauty. All of the boys wanted her. Many of the girls were jealous of her and, in the way of teenagers, were often petty and mean.

But Darcy was a tough cookie—she had to be to survive—and she didn't tolerate bullies. Trevor Ponce, one of her classmates, recalls the time in middle school when she received a school suspension for punching Mark Salas, the class bully who stole Trevor's new iPod. When I spoke to Trevor via phone, it was obvious he still looked up to Darcy as a hero. All of the outcasts did because she stood up for them when nobody else would.

"She was cool," Trevor said. "But not like in the same way as the popular kids. She didn't try to be—she just was. Effortlessly."

Even Mark Salas, now a CEO, came to respect her: "Everyone knew you didn't mess with her. She'd take you down and not think twice about it, but she'd also have your back if you needed her to."

Darcy made okay grades in school, but teachers often said she could've done better if she'd applied herself. She didn't participate in sports or after-school clubs. She was fine with admirers, but she didn't want friends. All she wanted was *out*.

Out of the cliquey school.

Out of the shabby trailer she lived in.

Out of the small town of Steam Valley, California.

But she never got the chance to leave.

On the chilly, windy night of October 26, 2007, Darcy's on-again, off-again boyfriend, Donovan Scott, convinced her to go to Hidden Beach—a difficult-to-access strip of sand tucked away in a cove, where local kids often had parties. It was their senior year, and the roughly one-hundred students from Redwood Coast High's Class of 2008 had a mean case of senioritis. There were parties every weekend, and this weekend was no exception. The teens lit a bonfire, drank cheap beer and wine coolers, reminisced about the last three years, and wondered what life would be like after high school.

Darcy hated it. By all accounts, she wanted to leave within minutes of arriving. Her boyfriend wanted to stay and drank heavily, ignoring her pleas to take her home.

Around 1:30 AM, witnesses saw a fight break out between Darcy and Donovan, a troubled kid from a troubled home with a hair-trigger temper. She reportedly slapped him and ran off into the vast wilderness of the Northern California redwoods. Drunk and angry, he followed her.

She was never seen again.

Fifteen years later, Darcy Megan Cantrell is famous. She's an urban legend local kids tell each other around a campfire on Hidden Beach. She's a ghost story, an unsolved mystery that has plagued law enforcement for years. But ask anyone in town, and they'll tell you the cold truth: she was murdered, and they know *exactly* who got away with it.

So, what really happened to Darcy? Did she finally run away as she'd always dreamed? Did she get lost on her way home and succumb to exposure in the rugged mountains? Or did something more sinister happen? And if she died that night, is Donovan to blame, or were there other suspects who were never investigated?

One thing's for sure—this case is anything but simple.

Stick with me this season as we delve deep into Darcy's story to see if we can uncover what really happened to her.

In the meantime, make sure to hit that subscribe button so you don't miss out on any future episodes of Cold Truth.

And, as always, if you have any information that could help solve this case or the others we've discussed, please don't hesitate to reach out.

Until next time—stay safe, stay curious, and never stop seeking the truth.

chapter
one

"FIGURED YOU'D BE HERE."

Donovan Scott bit back a growl of annoyance as his former best friend and current pain-in-the-ass boss emerged from the winding path onto the beach. He picked up the stick his border collie, Spirit, dropped at his feet and gave it a hard toss. She streaked after it in a blur of black and white and endless energy. "You wasted your time tracking me down. I'm not going to that fucking costume party."

"It's not a costume party. It's a masquerade ball," Zak Hendricks said as he crossed the sand. His dog, Ranger, raced out in front of him to join Spirit in the surf. "I'm assured there's a difference. And, yes, you're going."

"What are you going to do, Leg-o-less. Carry me there?"

"If I have to. My wife wants all of Redwood Coast Rescue in attendance. The *whole* team, and, like it or not, you became part of the team when you accepted Spirit's leash." Zak stopped next to where he sat in the sand and watched the dogs play. "She's doing well?"

"She's perfect." Nobody would know Spirit had a benign

tumor removed from her brain six months ago. It had affected her balance and ability to walk, but she recovered fast as soon as it was gone. Now she was a happy, healthy dog who loved to run and lived to sniff out explosive materials for a bite of her favorite treat: hot dogs. She was originally supposed to be a search and rescue K9, but her knack for bomb detection had been a welcome surprise since Donovan would've made a shitty SAR K9 handler. Explosives, he knew. He had been an EOD tech in the Marines, and even though he'd gotten himself blown up, he still liked bombs better than people. In his experience, they were less volatile.

"No more dizzy spells?"

He didn't know if Zak was asking about him or his dog, so he kept his mouth shut and his gaze focused on Spirit. Still, he could see the shine of Zak's prosthetic leg out of the corner of his eye. While the guy seemed to have accepted the disability now, it was an uncomfortable reminder of how broken the whole so-called team was.

Of how broken Donovan, himself, was.

Yeah, he had dizzy spells. They were happening more frequently, and there wasn't a damn thing he could do about it because his brain was Swiss cheese.

When he didn't respond, Zak turned to study the beach with a faint smile. "Lots of memories here."

Donovan followed his gaze. The beach hadn't changed much since they partied here as kids. It was a fingernail of sand tucked against almost vertical cliffs. Someone long ago had dug the fire pit and pulled large driftwood logs up around it to use as seats. He could still see Darcy sitting on one of the logs, her arms crossed, her eyes flashing with hatred. That had always been the problem with her—her line between love and hate was razor-thin, and it was impossible to know which side you stood on at any given time.

Now, ashes smoldered in the pit, sending up a thin curl of

smoke. High schoolers had been here partying last night, but there was no other sign of their presence. That was one of the only hard and fast rules of Hidden Beach. You packed out what you brought in.

"Almost fifteen years," Zak said after several beats of silence.

"How the fuck would you know?" Anger heated his blood, and he welcomed it. Yeah, anger was so much better than sorrow and regret. It was easier. Always had been. He supposed that was the problem with him and why he and Darcy had been doomed from the start. "Weren't you off saving the world or some shit when it happened?"

Zak had graduated the year before and was already an Army Ranger deployed overseas when Darcy died, or else he might have been a suspect, too.

Or probably not.

Ash Rawlings, the third member of their Terrible Trio, had still been around town at the time—hell, he'd even been at the party that night with his high school girlfriend—and nobody ever considered him a suspect, despite his fling with Darcy the previous summer. But Zak and Ash were both from upstanding, well-respected families. Zak's mom was the high school principal, and his dad was the history teacher and the lacrosse coach who led the Wildcats to the state championship multiple times. Ash was the heir of the town's founding family. The two of them always got away with everything, receiving little more than a slap on the wrist for their teenage troublemaking.

Donovan, as the kid from the wrong side of the tracks, never had that luxury. When they got a scolding, he got a beating. When they were grounded, he was tossed in county jail. It was part of the reason he'd grown to hate his former best friends over the years.

Zak's lips flattened into a grim line. "C'mon, Van. Everyone knows about Darcy's murder."

Donovan growled. "That fucking podcast."

"It started long before the podcast, buddy."

"Yeah, but it's stirring up all this shit again."

Zak said nothing. He just stared out over the waves.

"I didn't kill her."

"Never thought you did."

"Then you're the only one in this goddamn town to think that. If you want people to fork out money at this fundraiser shindig, you'd be better off not inviting the town pariah."

Zak finally glanced over at him again, one brow arched. "So why come back here at all? You could've lived anywhere after your medical discharge. You didn't have to come home."

Because his mom needed him. But Zak had been estranged from his family until recently and wouldn't understand that reasoning. "Because I'm a masochist."

"Then think of the charity ball tonight as another form of self-torture."

Fuck, he'd walked right into that, hadn't he? He stood and brushed sand off the back of his jeans. "I'm not wearing a costume."

Zak grinned. "Oh, yeah, you are."

chapter
two

TONIGHT WAS THE NIGHT.

Sasha LeBlanc was going to seduce a man for the first time in her life.

After years of crushing on Sheriff Ash Rawlings, she was finally going to make her move. Anna Hendricks, her best friend and Ash's twin sister, convinced her it was the only way anything would ever happen because Ash was too focused on keeping the citizens of Lost County safe to think about dating.

A hard worker. A good man.

He checked all the right boxes—kind, stable, good family, steady job. It was just a bonus he was also gorgeous. Stormy blue eyes. A square, too-serious face. He was from a long line of cattle ranchers and had the lean, strong body of a cowboy. She loved when he helped his sister around the rescue because he always rolled up his sleeves, showing off muscular arms sprinkled with dark hair. She had a weakness for men with sexy arms. He also had nice lips, the bottom fuller than the top, and the few times she'd seen him smile, he'd stolen her breath. While his sister's hair was a flaming copper, his neatly trimmed light brown hair and beard glinted with just a hint of red in the sun.

The perfect man.

At least, he was according to the life plan Sasha had meticulously plotted out for herself. She'd accomplished everything else on her list, so it was time to find a good husband and have a family, and she couldn't think of anyone better for the role than Ash Rawlings.

Luckily, Anna happened to agree and had been trying to play matchmaker for over a year now.

And tonight was finally the night.

Sasha studied her reflection in the full-length mirror. The silky black dress was like nothing she'd ever worn before. It shimmered faintly purple every time she moved, had a slit in the curve-hugging skirt almost up to her hip, and another plunged alarmingly between her breasts. A sheer cape spilled down her back from the shoulders and also sparkled with every movement.

Would Ash like it? He seemed like a very reserved man. A gentleman. Maybe she was showing too much skin.

"I don't know. Is it too much?"

Anna looked up from the tabletop mirror she was using to do her hair. She'd curled her copper hair and pulled it back into a complicated knot secured with jeweled pins that matched her deep blue dress. The elaborate blue and gold feathered bird mask she planned to wear sat on the vanity beside her and seemed to wink at Sasha.

"Honestly," Anna said after a contemplative beat, "I don't think it's enough."

"I don't want Ash to think I'm—" She broke off and glanced at Anna's seventeen-year-old foster daughter, Bella, who was sorting through a makeup kit on the bed. She was never sure how much she could say around the girl. Bella had lived a hard life and was more world wary than most teenagers, but she was still just a kid. Should they really be discussing this in front of her?

Bella smirked. "You don't want him to think you're what, sexy? Well, you should because when he sees you in that dress, his head's going to explode."

Flushing, Sasha turned back to the mirror. "I don't want him to think I'm easy."

"You're trying to seduce him, right?"

Sasha looked at her best friend for help, but Anna only shrugged.

"She's not wrong, Sash. My brother is a lot of things, but he's not a monk. He likes easy. Prefers it, in fact."

Was her face on fire? Because it felt like it was on fire. She was so far out of her comfort zone with the dress. With seduction. With... this whole plan. But she wasn't going to find a husband while buried in work at her vet clinic, though she would rather express a hundred anal glands—easily her most hated part of the job—than go to a party and seduce a man.

Stick to the plan.

That had been her mantra throughout her life.

Everything will be okay if you stick to the plan.

Her carefully curated life checklist had never failed her, so she just had to suck it up because she'd decided months ago that Ash was meant to be part of the plan.

And suck it in because, God, this dress clung to everything. She turned sideways and studied her profile in the mirror, smoothing her hands over her belly. She inhaled, but it was no use. "Are you sure I shouldn't wear Spanx?"

"I thought you wanted him to get you *out* of the dress tonight?" Anna asked.

"Spanx is *not* sexy," Bella added.

"But it shows a lot of... lumps."

"Honey, no." Anna sighed with obvious exasperation. "Those aren't lumps. Those are curves that most women would pay good money for—me included—and you got them naturally. Show them off!"

Sasha exhaled and turned away from the mirror. "I wish I could've lost more weight."

"You don't need to." Anna grabbed her shoulders and made her face the mirror again. "Look at you. You're *gorgeous*."

"Like a film noir femme fatale," Bella said. "Oh, wait!" She rifled through the massive makeup kit in front of her. She'd recently taken an interest in special effects, and Anna had encouraged the hobby by practically buying out the nearest Sephora. The girl had been through a lot in her young life, and even after finding a safe place to land with Zak and Anna, she'd struggled. She didn't trust easily. She was behind in school and had trouble making friends.

Sasha remembered how that felt. Whenever she looked at Bella, she saw an echo of her teenage self—the whole reason for her meticulous plan. Did Bella have a checklist, too? Or was she normal?

Bella held up a tube of dark red, almost black, lipstick. "You *have* to wear this."

No, it was too bold. Too dark. With her extremely fair skin and dark hair, the lipstick would probably make her look all pale and washed out like Wednesday Addams—a taunt she'd endured throughout high school—but Bella looked so hopeful holding it out, she couldn't say no. She dutifully applied it. The color was matte and made her lips look somehow bigger, and... okay, Bella was right. It did bring a glamorous old Hollywood vibe to her costume.

"Perfect," Anna said. "Now, the hair. What do you think, Belle?"

Bella got off the bed and circled Sasha, eyeing her up and down. "We'll lean into the femme fatale look and sweep it back, fluff it out, pin it up like in those old movies."

Anna grinned. "With your mask on, nobody will recognize you."

That's the point.

As Anna and Bella worked magic with her thick mass of hair, she tried to imagine she was someone other than a shy, awkward, overweight veterinarian. She was Greta Garbo. Rita Hayworth. Ava Gardner. She was beautiful, glamorous, and mysterious. She was...

Going to be sick.

"This isn't going to work."

"Yes, it will. I know my brother. He won't be able to resist you." Anna crossed to the bottle of champagne she'd had chilling in a bucket in the corner of the bedroom and popped the cork. She returned with two bubbling glasses. "What you need is a little liquid courage."

Sasha accepted the glass with a shaking hand and clinked it with Anna's, then downed it in three long swallows.

"Yikes," Bella said. "It's gonna take *a lot* of liquid courage, Mom."

"Yeah, I see that." Anna took the empty glass back and refilled it. "Good thing I bought two bottles."

chapter
three

THE MASQUERADE BALL was held in a rented ballroom at River's Edge Casino, and Zak had left hours ago to coordinate the set-up while Anna and Sasha got ready. Bella drove them to the casino since they'd polished off most of the champagne before ever leaving the house.

Sasha's head felt floaty, as bubbly as the champagne, and she couldn't stop smiling. Her cheeks were probably flushed—they always got red when she drank—but at least she had the lacy Venetian mask to hide that.

"Be good," Bella said as she dropped them off at the casino's entrance.

"I'm supposed to be telling *you* that," Anna said.

"But I didn't pregame with an entire bottle of champagne, and I'm spending my night watching Disney movies with Poppy and Grandma Paksima. So I'm telling *you* to be good."

Anna laughed and leaned back into the car to kiss Bella's forehead. "Give that to Poppy." She added a second kiss. "And that's for you. Let me know when you get to your grandparents' house."

"I will. Bye, Mom. Love you!"

"Love you, too." Anna stepped back and exhaled long and

slow as she watched the car until it had turned out of the parking lot. Tears brimmed in her eyes. "Oh, no. Oh, shit. I can't cry. I'll ruin the fabulous job Bella did on my makeup."

Sasha hooked her arm and leaned into her side, offering support. "Is that the first time she's said she loves you?"

"Yes." Anna's lips trembled. "Poppy says it all the time, but I didn't think Bella ever would."

Sasha thought of the precocious six-year-old with blond hair and enormous blue eyes that Zak and Anna had officially adopted six months ago. The girl was as bright and happy as her name suggested, and a lot of that had to do with Bella shielding her from the worst of their shared trauma. The girls were raised as sisters, but they weren't blood-related. Due to a lot of complicated circumstances, Zak and Anna hadn't been able to adopt Bella like they had Poppy, who was an orphan, so they were still only the older girl's foster parents. And Bella was about to turn eighteen, aging her out of the traditional foster system and into a transitional group home. Sasha knew Zak and Anna were desperately jumping through all the legal hoops to adopt her before that happened.

"Poppy had a lot less trauma to work through than Bella."

"Because Bella is so smart and strong and resilient. She's such a good kid. And now I just want to protect them both from all of it." Anna started to wipe at the tears in her eyes but caught herself. "Dammit. I'm *not* going to cry. Tonight's a good night. A happy night."

Sasha turned her toward the casino's door. "Exactly. No tears. You'll go in there and dance with your handsome husband and have fun while you raise boatloads of money for our rescue."

Anna gave a watery laugh. "Well, I don't know about boat-loads, but the ticket sales were beyond anything we expected. With any luck, the silent auction and donations will put us over the top of our stretch goal."

"*Boatloads* of money," Sasha insisted.

"Yeah, okay. Boatloads." She gave a sly sideways smile. "And you, my friend, are going to snag yourself a handsome sheriff tonight, and then we'll be sisters."

The nerves fluttered again, and Sasha pressed her free hand to her belly. "Maybe don't start sending the wedding invitations just yet. He has to notice me first."

"Oh, he will. *Everyone* will. Believe me, Sash, you look amazing."

The ballroom was filled with a cacophony of colors and textures. Anna had outdone herself with the decorations. An expansive buffet of delicious treats and appetizers lined one wall, and a bar was tucked away in the corner. On the stage in front of the dance floor, a small jazz band played a lively tune, electrifying the air. Many of the masqueraders mingled among the high-top cocktail tables in shimmering fabrics and intricate masks of feathers and sequins. Others had already taken to the dance floor, laughing in their partners' arms. Overhead, chandeliers cascaded droplets of light into the crowd below.

Anna wasn't over-exaggerating the number of ticket sales. It looked like the entire town had turned up to support Redwood Coast Rescue, and Sasha's heart swelled at the thought. Zak and Anna had worked hard to make RWCR an asset to the community, and people were finally taking notice.

The night felt alive with possibility.

"Oh, there's Zak." Anna pulled her toward one of the tables, where Zak stood with Pierce St. James and Sawyer Murphy, two other members of Redwood Coast Rescue's tactical K9 unit. Pierce wore a plain black mask that covered the lower half of his face and the extensive scars on his neck, and Sawyer had on an eyeless cyberpunk mask that made him look like an android. Even Zelda, Sawyer's seeing-eye dog, was dressed to impress in a silver tutu that sparkled with green twinkle lights.

"Ladies," Sawyer said with a gallant bow. "I'd say you look beautiful, but I'm blinder than usual tonight." He grinned as he tapped his eyeless mask. "But I bet you're both putting every other woman to shame."

Pierce said something in sign language. He was unable to speak due to injuries he received while serving in Iraq. Sasha had been trying to learn to sign so she could talk with him, but she didn't know enough of the language yet to translate what he said.

"Yeah, don't get any ideas," Zak replied and pulled Anna possessively into his side. While the two other men simply wore tuxes with their masks, he had gone full pirate with his costume, even replacing his usual prosthetic running blade with a peg leg. He cut a dashing figure in the long red jacket with gold trim. A huge tricorn hat sat at a jaunty angle on his head, and his half-mask was a freakishly realistic gold skull.

In a past life, he absolutely had been a pirate, Sasha decided. He looked too much the part to have been anything else.

"Wow," he said and gave his wife an appreciative spin. "Look at you, gorgeous. My favorite parrot."

She poked his chest. "I better be your *only* parrot."

Aww, they'd coordinated. Now Anna's bird-like costume made a lot more sense.

Sasha glanced away from the couple as they kissed, a hollow ache blooming in her heart. She wanted what they had —that sweet, easy intimacy with someone who saw all her flaws and accepted her anyway. She scanned the crowd for Ash, but she couldn't pick him out of the sea of jesters and plague doctors. Her gaze snagged on a man in the corner dressed all in black, his silk shirt loosely laced at the collar, showing off impressively wide shoulders and the hint of a tattoo on his chest. His demon mask completely covered his face, leaving just his square jaw and dimpled chin visible. Definitely not Ash because he didn't have a beard, but she found herself watching him a beat too long anyway. He lifted his drink in her direction, and she realized she was staring.

Oh, shit. Now she'd have to avoid Demon Man all night.

Face burning, she turned away from him and accepted a glass of champagne from a passing waiter. Her head was already fuzzy from the bottles she'd shared with Anna, but she needed to quiet the damn nerves fluttering in her belly. As she sipped, she continued scanning the crowd, but she was still too aware of Demon Man's gaze on her.

She had to focus.

She was on a mission.

She took another sip of champagne. She needed to find Ash, and fast, before she lost the nerve. But where was he? She should've asked Anna what his costume was. Perhaps he opted not to come to the party after all.

Her gaze found its way back to Demon Man, who was now stalking across the room toward her. She tried to look away but found that she couldn't.

"May I have this dance?" he asked, holding out his hand. He was a perfect gentleman, but she hesitated and stared down at his extended hand. It was big and powerful and somehow menacing. She imagined it spread possessively across her lower back. Then imagined it sliding lower...

Maybe it was the anonymity of the masks they both wore that made her feel bold, or maybe it was the champagne fizzing her blood, but she placed her hand in his and allowed him to lead her out onto the dance floor.

She wasn't a dancer. Nobody would ever call her graceful, but she easily fell into the rhythm of the lively music with him. The man could *move,* and it was sexy as hell. Who knew she was attracted to men who could dance? She sure hadn't.

Soon enough, she stopped worrying about his hands skimming over the lumps and bumps her dress didn't hide. She stopped worrying if she was going to step on his foot. She laughed as he spun her out and back in. It was kind of... fun.

God. When was the last time she'd let herself have fun?

As the music slowed, his muscular arms wrapped around her waist and tugged her close. Her face flushed with heat, and this time it had nothing to do with the champagne. It was a pleasant warmth that spread throughout her body to tingle in her fingers and toes. This wasn't part of the plan, but as she stared up at his masked face, she found herself losing all sense of reason. Dancing with a stranger in a demon mask was so out of character, but she wasn't ready to stop. It was too exciting. Exhilarating.

And yet, even as they danced, she couldn't shake the feeling that someone was watching her.

It wasn't until the dance ended and Demon Man pulled away from her that she finally saw him. Ash. He was standing near the door, dressed in a simple black cloak, talking to Zak. He looked like a shadow in the dimly lit room, but she knew it was him. He still had his Lost County Sheriff's uniform on under the hastily donned cloak. Probably Anna's doing. She wouldn't let anyone— even her brother—enter without a costume.

Sasha's heart skipped a beat as she realized what she had just done. She had danced with this dangerous stranger while Ash—the perfect man, the one who checked all of the boxes in her tidy life plan—had been there all along.

Dammit, she had to focus.

The plan was to seduce Ash, not Demon Man.

Stick to the plan.

"Thank you. That was fun, but—" She tried to extricate herself gracefully, but Demon Man caught her hand.

"Where are you going?" His voice was a low rumble that sent sparks through her nerve endings as he drew her in close. "I'm not done with you yet."

"I... uh... need to go." A faint protest, her voice barely above a whisper. She could see his dark eyes burning with intensity under the mask and found herself almost hypnotized by his gaze. "I was waiting for a friend, and he's here now, so—"

"Forget him." He leaned in closer, his breath hot against her ear. "Come with me."

It was a mistake, but she didn't protest again as he led her away from the crowd and into a darkened corner of the room. Demon Man trapped her against the velvet-draped wall with his big body, and his stubble scraped her cheek as his lips hovered inches above hers. His hand curled loosely around her neck, his thumb tracing her collarbone up to her fluttering pulse.

But he didn't kiss her.

God, she wanted him to kiss her.

Her hand automatically came up to his shoulder as if she meant to push him away, but then slid down his tattooed arm. Fascinated, she traced the lines of ink carved into his skin with her fingertips. His muscles tightened under her touch.

He made a sound of pure male need, deep and primal. His hands slid down to her hips, then around to her ass. He pulled her against him, and there was no mistaking his arousal. The ridge of it pressed against her stomach as he skimmed his lips from the corner of her mouth to her neck. He breathed in deeply as if trying to inhale her like a drug.

She was in trouble. She was veering way off her predetermined route here, but what would it hurt just this once? Then she could go back to checking off boxes on her tidy plan.

No.

No.

Her eyes popped open in shock. Those wayward thoughts had to be the champagne talking. This man was *not* part of her plan. When she went off plan, bad things happened. The last time, she'd lost the most important person in the world to her.

Never again.

She forced herself to step back.

He growled softly and stepped forward, crowding her against the wall. She pressed her hand to his chest and felt his heart beating as hard as hers under her palm.

"I have to go," she said again, more firmly.

Demon Man didn't reply right away, but the stubborn look in his eyes said he wasn't ready to give up on her, and he was debating how hard he should push. And, if she were honest with herself, it wouldn't take much of a push. She was insanely attracted to this man—more attracted than she had been to anyone—and she hadn't even seen his entire face yet.

He was dangerous.

So, so dangerous.

After several breathless beats, he leaned in close, and his lips brushed her ear. "Find me later," he whispered before backing away and disappearing into the crowd.

Sasha stood there for a moment, her heart racing as she tried to remember how to breathe.

What just happened?

And why did she want to follow him now?

Yeah, that definitely had to be the champagne's influence.

chapter
four

SHE CAUGHT sight of Ash again, and she knew what she had to do.

Stick. To. The. Plan.

Time to go for what she wanted. If she could sizzle on the dance floor with a stranger, she could be bold enough to ask Ash on a date.

She threw back her shoulders, lifted her chin, and made her way over to him. She tapped his shoulder. "Hi," she said, trying to keep her voice steady. "I've been looking for you."

Ash turned to face her, his eyes widening in surprise as he took in her dress. "Sasha?" The surprise shifted to appreciation, then into the spark of male interest she'd always wanted from him. A smile spread across his handsome face. "Wow. You look... amazing."

"I like you. I think we'd make a great couple. Would you date me?" The words fell out of her in a jumbled rush on one breath. Crap. She inwardly winced. There was a line between boldness and tactlessness, and she just took a running leap over it. "Um, I mean... dance with me?"

Ash glanced at his companions, and her face went hot as she

realized she didn't know the men standing with him. Which was worse—embarrassing yourself in front of strangers or friends? She wanted to melt into the floor and suddenly, desperately wished she'd taken Demon Man up on his offer to leave.

"Yeah, I'd love to dance with you," Ash said, surprising her. "Just give me a second?"

"Oh. Right. Of course."

He turned back to the two men. They were dressed similarly to him, with uniforms under their cloaks. His deputies, she realized. They were trying to keep the grins off their faces and remain professional.

Oh, God. She wandered away while Ash issued their orders. Her face was on fire, and her nerves were back. She snagged another champagne glass from a passing waiter. Funny how she hadn't felt even a hint of the nervous butterflies when she'd danced with Demon Man.

Then Ash's hand was in hers, and he was leading her to the dance floor. Her heart pounded so hard in her chest that she was sure he could feel it through their clasped hands.

This was it. The moment she had been waiting for. The moment she had planned for.

She drew a breath to calm her racing thoughts and focus on the moment as he took her into his arms, but from the corner of her eye, she saw his deputies fan out into the crowd. "Are you working?"

"No," Ash said too quickly.

"You're in uniform. You only wear your uniform when there's a problem." Otherwise, he usually wore jeans and a button-up to work. "What's wrong?"

He exhaled hard. "Okay, yes, I'm working. But don't tell Anna. One: she'll lecture me about always working. And two: I don't want her to worry."

"Worry about what?"

"We received information about a potential attack on the fundraiser tonight."

"Who would attack a fundraiser?" Her eyes widened. "Monarch?" Anna was in an intense legal battle with the development company over land that had been owned by the Rawlings family since the Gold Rush days. "They wouldn't stoop that low."

"I wouldn't put it past them," Ash muttered but then nodded toward two men in expensive tuxes and simple black masks. "But Mark Salas and JT Tennison are both here, so I doubt it's them."

She scowled at the Monarch CEO and Chief Legal Officer. "Why would they buy tickets to a fundraiser meant to raise money to fight them?"

"Because JT's a sycophant who worships the ground Mark walks on, and Mark's a smug jackass. Always was in high school, and he's only gotten worse with age and success."

She was a year younger than Ash and had kept to herself throughout school, preferring to focus on her grades rather than social events. They hadn't run with the same crowd, but she did vaguely remember Mark ruling over his classmates as prom king, like the position actually came with God-given monarchal power. "He always wore polo shirts with popped collars."

"He still does, if that tells you anything."

"Ew." Then a thought struck that had her jaw falling open. "Wait. Did he name his company Monarch because he was elected prom king?"

Ash laughed. It was a deep, rich sound. "You know, I never thought of that, but probably."

"Wow, that's really pathetic."

"Pathetic is a good word to describe Mark, but he's not the kind of guy who's going to call in a bomb threat. He prefers to sue people to get his way."

"So, who would threaten the fundraiser?"

He lifted a shoulder in a shrug. "Probably just kids, but I'm not taking any chances. I have deputies stationed at every door and a bomb-sniffing K9 unit from the state police patrolling the grounds. Like I said, it's probably nothing, but this is my sister's baby. I'm not taking chances."

She loved that he cared so much about Anna and her many passion projects. His protectiveness was sweet.

The music slowed, and Ash pulled her closer. He smelled nice, like the woods after a rain, and she relaxed into his arms. He was a good dancer, his touch gentle but confident.

Nothing like Demon Man, who had been all rough edges and primitive need. That was what made him so dangerous—his unpredictability, his wildness. Ash was safe, reliable—a good choice for a life partner.

But was that really what she wanted?

Yes.

Yes, of course.

Safe and reliable was better.

And while she couldn't deny that the dance with Demon Man had been the most exciting thing she'd ever done, she couldn't risk another deviation from her plan. She'd lost too much already.

As if conjured by her thoughts, Demon Man appeared at the edge of the dance floor. He still wore his mask, but she could tell by the flat line of his mouth that he disapproved of her current dance partner. His dark eyes all but burned her skin. Her heart thundered as she met his gaze over Ash's shoulder, torn between Ash, the safe choice, and Demon Man, the wild card.

Dammit, it shouldn't even be a debate. She shouldn't be looking at him. Shouldn't be entertaining the idea of leaving Ash after this next dance and going to him—but she couldn't help it. There was something about him that drew her in, something magnetic that made her feel more alive than she had in years.

She imagined that was how bugs felt right before they got zapped.

When the song ended, Ash didn't let her go. She pulled her gaze away from Demon Man and made herself focus on Ash. He leaned down, his breath warm against her cheek, and for a heart-stopping moment, she thought he was going to kiss her.

Did she want him to kiss her?

Yes.

No.

"Anna's watching," he said, his voice a sexy rumble in her ear.

Sasha glanced over at her best friend, who gave her an enthusiastic thumbs up. She laughed and buried her burning face in Ash's shoulder. "Oh my God. She looks like the Cheshire Cat."

He grumbled low in his throat, but it was good-natured. "She's very pleased with herself right now. She's been telling me to ask you out for years." He pushed a loose strand of hair back from her face and smiled. "I'm an idiot for not listening to her sooner."

The nerves swarmed back. "Oh. Well, uh, don't tell her that, or you'll never hear the end of it."

The radio at his belt squawked with chatter. He cursed under his breath before letting her go. "Sorry, I have to—"

"No, don't apologize. I get it. I'm always on call, too." The nearest emergency animal hospital was almost two hours away, and sometimes a patient just didn't have that long. She and two other vets in town took turns being on call for emergencies, and it wasn't unusual for the answering service to contact her at all hours of the night.

Ash walked backward a few steps, seemingly reluctant to

leave. "Do you want to get dinner sometime when I'm not..." He trailed off and waved vaguely in the direction of his deputies, who were both trying to get his attention. "You know, being pulled in five directions at once?"

She hesitated, glancing over at Demon Man. He was still watching her, his eyes dark and intense. It was as if he was daring her to come to him, to embrace the danger that he represented.

But she couldn't do that. She had to stick to the safe and reliable choice.

She faced Ash again. "Yes, I'd like that."

He smiled, relief evident in his expression. "Great. Call you tomorrow?"

"Okay," she said faintly.

With a final, quick smile—he really was handsome when he did that—he jogged off to answer the radio and deal with his deputies, leaving her alone on the dance floor with her racing thoughts.

She'd finally done it. She got Ash to notice her. So why did she have knots in her stomach?

She took a deep breath and turned to go find Anna—and nearly ran into Demon Man. He was right there, crowding her space, and she didn't care. The uneasy knots loosened.

"Hi," she whispered.

"Dance we me," he said, his voice low and rough.

Her gaze flicked over to where Anna was standing, hoping for an intervention to stop her from making a horrible decision.

Anna wasn't there anymore.

Crap.

She stared up at the contours of his mask, the sharp angles that gave him an imposing air. She knew she should say no and walk away, but something inside her wouldn't let her. Maybe it was the thrill of the danger, the excitement of the unknown.

Maybe it was the way he made her feel when they danced, like she was the center of his world.

Whatever it was, she couldn't resist.

And then the decision was made for her as he took her hand and pulled her close. The music had started again, a sultry, sinuous beat that matched the way Demon Man moved against her. He was all rough edges and primal need, his hands gripping her waist as he dipped her low, his face so close to hers that she could feel his breath on her lips.

She should push him away, should tell him to stop, but she couldn't find the words. She felt like she was caught in a spell, her body moving in perfect sync with his. It was too much, too intense.

"You're dangerous, you know that?"

"That's why you like me," he said with a wicked grin as his big hands roamed over her butt. "You want to feel something real. Something wild."

Yes, it was true. She'd always wanted to be the kind of person who embraced adventure and thrived on the unexpected. He could help her unlock that side of herself if she let him. There was no safety net with him, no plan to follow, no neat little checkboxes to mark off.

It was thrilling.

And terrifying.

As they moved together, she allowed herself to be swept away by his touch, his lips, his blatantly carnal energy.

Suddenly, he spun her out and pulled her back tight to him, his hand trailing down her spine as the music reached its crescendo. He was aroused. She could feel the bulge of his erection pressing into her stomach, and dampness pooled uncomfortably between her thighs.

He growled softly. "You want me, don't you?"

She should deny it, but she couldn't. The heat between them was too intense. She nodded just as the music ended.

"Then come with me."

Sasha hesitated and looked for Ash. He was gone. Anna was gone. Even Zak. Nobody would see her sneak away with this man. Her mind screamed that it wasn't a good idea, but her body had already made its decision. She felt daring with him—like she could do anything. It was a heady feeling. Dangerous. But, at that moment, she didn't care.

chapter
five

SASHA'S PULSE quickened as he held out his hand. His eyes danced with amusement behind his mask, and at that moment, he truly looked demonic. She should refuse the temptation. She should leave his arms and wait for Ash, because he was the right man for her, not this stranger who set her on fire with just his touch. She had to say no. She had to be smart, stick to her plan. It hadn't failed her yet—

She nodded.

His lips twitched into a smile as his hand wrapped around hers, his grip firm and warm. For a moment, she forgot everything else as they walked together toward the door leading out to the casino floor.

He took a keycard from his pocket.

He had a room at the hotel.

Her heart raced while they waited for an elevator. She was both trembling in anticipation and filled with trepidation as the doors opened and they stepped inside.

Was she really going to do this?

She sneaked a glance at him, at his strong jaw and the muscles that strained his shirt and his big hands. Anticipation zinged through her.

Yes, she was really doing this.

The elevator ride lasted forever and not long enough, the space between them crackling with electricity. He said nothing, and other than his hand around hers, he didn't touch her again until they were safely inside his room. Then he pushed her up against the closed door and fastened his mouth over hers, hungry as if he'd been dying for a taste of her all night. He held her still while he commanded her mouth, and all she could do was stand there and melt under the siege.

When she was breathless, he finally released her face and gripped her hips, hauling her hard against him as if to imprint himself on her skin. She dug her fingers into the sinewy muscles of his forearms and wrapped her leg around him, pulling him even closer so there would be no space between them. His kiss alone was enough reason to stay—he was wild and hot, just as she imagined.

He broke away from her mouth to trail his lips down her neck. She tilted her head back, giving him better access to the sensitive skin. He bit down gently, eliciting a husky moan that startled her. She didn't make sounds like that, but he seemed to like it. He grabbed her ass and lifted her up like she didn't weigh over two hundred pounds.

She squeaked in surprise. "Oh my God. Put me down. You'll hurt yourself."

His dark, amused chuckle sent shivers racing over her skin. "I want both your legs around me."

She tried to obey, but the dress was too tight. Embarrassment stung her cheeks. "Uh, I can't. My dress—"

With a frustrated growl, he set her down long enough to reach around her. But instead of the zipper sound she expected, the fabric tore. She gasped into his mouth as the dress fell off her, ripped nearly in two. Then he had her in his arms again, and her legs were wrapped around his waist as he carried her to the bed. He lay her down and hovered over her, his eyes locked onto hers. He still wore the demon mask, and the illicitness of it sent a thrill through her.

His thumb stroked over her lower lip. "I'm only asking this once. Are you sure?"

She nodded. She was going to combust if he didn't keep touching her. She reached up to pull him down for another kiss, their lips meeting in a fierce battle of tongues. His hands roamed over her body, leaving trails of fire. He hooked his fingers into her thong and dragged it down.

For once, she wasn't self-conscious about her belly or her muffin top or her jiggly thighs. How could she be when he worshiped her with his hands and mouth like she was a goddess?

As they broke away for air, he murmured in her ear, "You're mine now."

She nodded again, her eyes wide as she watched him rise from the bed. He took his time unlacing the shirt at his collar and shrugged it off, revealing a thickly muscled chest. Dark tattoos snaked from his powerful shoulders, down both arms to his wrists. He tossed the shirt aside before nudging off his boots.

When he reached to take off the mask, she sat up and grabbed his hand. "Leave it. Please."

He leaned down, his lips hovering above hers. "Does the angel want to be fucked by the demon?"

A chill scraped down her spine. Her nipples hardened, poking through the thin lace of her bra. "Yes."

He left the mask in place and held her gaze as he unzipped his pants. She watched with amazement as he pushed them down his powerful thighs and kicked them away. His cock was thick and long, and her mouth watered at the sight of it. On impulse, she reached out, wrapped her hand around the heavy length of him, and squeezed. She had no idea where the boldness came from, but she liked feeling the power of him, the heat. Liked that she was in full control of this demon of a man, and they both knew it.

She stroked her hand up, squeezed, and then down again, watching his face. He closed his eyes and tipped his head back, his jaw tight with tension. She leaned forward to lick the hollow of his throat. His deep groan sent a rush of wetness between her thighs.

He gripped her head and kissed her hard. She wrapped her hand more tightly around him, moving up and down, then twisted her wrist to glide over the silky skin of his tip and back down once more.

With a growl, he caught her wrist. "Fuck, you're a naughty angel." His voice was ragged. "Not like that. I'm not coming in your hand. I want inside you."

He grabbed a condom from the bedside table and ripped it open with his teeth. She licked her lips, watching as he roughly rolled it on.

He positioned himself above her and leaned down to kiss her, his tongue tangled with hers as his knees pressed her legs apart. When he finally broke the kiss and positioned himself at her entrance, she let out a choked cry. He was so big. He pushed the head of his cock inside and paused. She looked up at him, trying desperately to catch her breath.

"I'm going to fuck you slow," he growled. "Because you're tight. And sweet. And I want to feel every inch of you. But when I'm close to coming, I'm going to shove myself in deep and fast." He thrust forward, and a whimper escaped her as her body accepted him. "And I'm going to come. Because I'm your demon, and that's what a demon does—he fucks and fucks you hard until he comes. And then he does it all over again."

She closed her eyes and tried to keep her breathing even. He was right. She hated it, and yet she loved it. She hated herself for liking what he was doing to her, but she loved the way he spoke of it.

As if he had done this to a thousand women before.

As if he did not have a soul.

When he began to move, she arched beneath him, digging her hands into his arms to pull him down on top of her. But he didn't give her what she wanted. He drew out almost all the way and then pushed back in, slower than before, a little deeper but still not all the way.

Every stroke shoved her closer to the edge. His chest rubbed against her nipples, sending little zings of pleasure down to where they were joined. She buried her face in his neck and gripped his hips, wanting him to move faster, deeper, harder.

But he kept up the torturously slow rhythm.

He kissed her again, his tongue tangling with hers, soft and demanding all at once. She wrapped her legs around his hips and pulled him closer. She was so close to the edge that she didn't know how she would survive.

He grabbed one of her hands and forced it to his mouth as he continued to move in and out of her, torturously slow. "Play with your clit, angel."

Her face grew warm as she slid her fingers down between her thighs. She gasped, embarrassed by the pleasure and the wetness. He stopped moving and withdrew her hand, licked the tip of her finger. She moaned softly as he replaced her hand on herself.

"Harder," he said.

She rubbed the bud harder, faster.

"You're so hot, angel," he said, punctuating each word with a thrust. "So fucking hot. I could stay inside you all night. All fucking night."

She moaned against his neck as another zing of pleasure shot through her. Her eyes squeezed shut and she arched against him, meeting his hard thrusts. She was so close, so close.

"That feels so fucking good. I know you're close, I can feel you squeezing. It's so fucking tight. Come on my cock, angel. It's time to come."

Her body obeyed, the orgasm hit her fast and hard. Her hips bucked up and she screamed against his neck as his cock slid so deep inside her she wildly thought she'd never get him out.

Then she couldn't think anymore as pleasure took over and the room spun. His movements grew rough, wild. He wrapped one hand over her hip and pulled her leg to his waist as he slammed into her over and over, jerky and uncontrolled. His grunts became deeper, yet he didn't slow down.

He stiffened above her, and she knew he was close.

He threw his head back, his neck muscles corded. In that moment, she could see the demon in him, and he was beautiful. She wrapped her hand around his neck, drawing him closer for another hard kiss as he finally came.

When they both stilled, he bit her neck. Then he licked the sting away and kissed the spot.

"What was that?" she rasped.

He shook his head. "Nothing, angel. I'm just marking you. Remember? It's what demons do."

He pulled out of her and took off the condom, leaving the bed to dispose of it in the bathroom.

When he returned, his eyes were heavy behind the demon mask. He pulled it off, and she glanced away. She didn't want to see his face and ruin the magic of what had just happened. It was better if they stayed strangers. He slid into bed behind her and pulled her back against his chest.

Oh, God. What had she done?

She started to get up, but his arms tightened around her.

His breath tickled the back of her neck. "Where do you think you're going?"

"I should go find my friends before they leave. They're my ride home."

"Oh, angel," he said, his voice dripping with mock sadness. "You'll stay here tonight. I'm not done with you."

He was already stirring again, lengthening against the back of her thigh, and her body hummed with anticipation, ready for round two.

She had no idea how she'd gotten herself into this mess. She was always so cautious, always planning ahead, and yet here she was in a stranger's bed, wanting more than she should. She wanted to stay with him, wanted to explore the depths of his eyes and the texture of the hair on his chest. She wanted to wrap her hand around his hardening cock again and taste him when he came.

But what if Anna was looking for her? Or worse, Ash? He definitely wouldn't want her after finding her in bed with someone else.

On one hand, she felt guilty for betraying her own convictions. But on the other, she couldn't help but be pulled in by his presence, captivated by the thrill of their embrace and the pleasure it brought her. She wanted more—more of the thrill, more of the pleasure, more of the passion.

"I should go home." But even as she said the words, she knew she wouldn't. She didn't want to leave her demon's embrace yet.

"Mmm. Stay." The seductive timbre of his voice sent chills of desire rippling through her body.

She hesitated. Would it be so bad if she stayed? This need for him didn't make sense. She never even asked his name.

"What's your name?" Her breath hitched as his rough hand trailed lightly down her hip.

He nuzzled her ear and dipped his fingers between her

legs. "Do you often have hot sex with men you don't know?" She couldn't tell if it was amusement or annoyance in his voice.

"No." She gasped and arched into him, pushing against his touch, desperate for more. "This is the first time."

His deep rumble of laughter resonated through her body as he began to trace circles around her aching clit. "But that's not true, is it? Because you *do* know me."

No, she didn't. She couldn't. She never would've done this with someone she knew because how could she face him every day with such intimate, carnal knowledge of his body?

He was a stranger.

He had to be.

She closed her eyes and grabbed his wrist with the intention of removing his hand, but didn't follow through. Instead, she let him continue to tantalize her with his skilled fingers. "No, I don't."

"Yes, you do. Say my name, Sasha." He continued to circle her clit as he waited for an answer, but instead of giving him one, all she could do was moan. His voice dropped low in anticipation. "C'mon, who's your demon? Say my name, and I'll let you come."

The pleasure was deep and relentless, but he held back just enough pressure to keep her from release until his name left her in a pleading gasp. "Donovan."

A triumphant growl rumbled from his chest. He sped up the movement of his hand, replacing his thumb with two fingers. "Say it again."

Desperate now, she cried out. "Donovan, please!"

He pinched her clit between his fingers, and the orgasm ripped through her like wildfire. She was still pulsing as he wrapped his arms around her and tucked her tight against him.

"That's right, angel," he murmured into her hair. "That's right. And you're mine now."

Oh, no. No, no, no. She couldn't be his. He wasn't part of the plan. Tonight was only meant to be a short, wild detour.

But even as the halfhearted denial crossed her mind, her body softened and molded against his. Her eyes drifted closed, and she gave in to the pull of a blissful, sated sleep.

episode 2: the search

Hey there, Truth Seekers! Welcome back to Cold Truth, the true-crime podcast that dives deep into the most challenging cold cases. I'm Alexis Summers, your host, and today we're continuing our investigation into the disappearance of Darcy Cantrell, the teenage girl who vanished without a trace. In our last episode, we explored Darcy's life. Now, we'll be examining the efforts made to find her and bring her home. So, grab your detective hats, and let's get into it!

Sheriff Jerald T. Tennison Sr., or Sheriff Jerry as he was known around Steam Valley, was a twenty-year veteran of the Lost County Sheriff's Department and in 2007, he'd recently won a hard-fought election to the sheriff's seat. On Halloween day, he was waiting in line at the local coffee house for his morning caffeine hit when he received a call about a missing teenage girl.

It had been five days since the party at Hidden Beach.

Nobody noticed Darcy was missing until she didn't show up for her waitressing shift at The Grove. The diner's owner, Gwenda Prescott, was instantly worried. It wasn't a secret that Darcy wanted to leave town, but she'd already made plans with Gwenda to stay and work full-time through the summer tourist season after graduation because she needed money. She showed up for every shift and often picked up extra hours before and after school. In the three years she'd worked for Gwenda, she'd called off only a handful of times and never no-called-no-showed. So when calls to her cell phone went unanswered, Gwenda decided to contact the police.

Law enforcement was very familiar with the Cantrell family. Sheriff Jerry had responded to many domestic disturbance calls at their trailer over the years and had been first on scene when Sissy overdosed. It was a rough environment for a child to grow up in, but nothing could be done since Sissy always refused to press charges against her husband, and Darcy never complained of abuse after her mother died, even though she often showed up to school with unexplained bruises.

So, of course, Sheriff Jerry's first thought was that Darcy had run away. Nobody would've been surprised if she'd decided to leave. At eighteen, she was legally an adult and could disappear if she wanted. The sheriff's office simply had to confirm that she'd left willingly, then they could close the case.

Franklin Cantrell was at sea and hadn't seen his daughter in nearly two weeks, but he gave his reluctant permission via radio for a search of the house—a search that would ultimately leave investigators with more questions than answers.

Darcy's suitcase was in the closet with a thin layer of dust on top, and she'd been in the middle of doing laundry. A load still moldered in the washer. Her purse was on her dresser, and inside, they found her cell phone and eighty dollars in ones and fives—tips from her Friday evening shift—along with her ID and debit card. They found more tip money stashed in a shoebox under her bed, totaling five hundred dollars, and bank statements that showed she had another thousand in savings. A call to Sheriff Jerry's wife at the credit union proved her account remained untouched.

If Darcy had left of her own accord, she'd at least have taken her money.

Where was she?

So, things start heating up in the search for Darcy Cantrell. Our trusty town sheriff is now on the case, talking with witnesses and retracing Darcy's last steps. He knew they were starting the search with a huge disadvantage. The first few days after a person disappears are the most critical—and Darcy had already been gone for nearly a week.

But it didn't take long before he noticed a pattern in the witness statements. One name kept popping up – none other than Donovan Scott, the town troublemaker. This guy's got a reputation a mile wide for causing chaos and getting into fights. Sheriff Jerry even threw him in jail a few months prior for vandalism, but the charges were dropped, and he walked away without punishment. Sounds like a solid first suspect, right? Especially since Donovan and Darcy were next-door neighbors and known to date.

So the sheriff headed over to Donovan's house. His mom claimed he wasn't home, but Sheriff Jerry was not convinced. He decided to wait it out, and sure enough, after a few hours, Donovan made a run for it out the back door. I mean, who does that? It's suspicious as hell. Did he really think he was going to get away?

So, they catch the kid and bring him in for questioning. At first, he's denying everything. He doesn't know Darcy that well. He's never been to Hidden Beach. He doesn't know anything about anything. But as Sheriff Jerry dug deeper, Donovan's story started to fall apart. He eventually admitted that he had attended the party at Hidden Beach with Darcy and that they had gotten into an argument. He claimed that Darcy had left the party on her own, and he hadn't seen her since. But the sheriff suspected the kid was lying through his teeth.

So, what does Sheriff Jerry do? He gets a search warrant, and investigators start combing through the Scott house. And let me tell you, what they found was disturbing. There were bloodstains on the underside of the carpet in the living room that someone had attempted to clean. And—get this—a baseball bat in Donovan's closet with traces of blood on it. Not looking good for Donovan, right? The kid was getting nervous and more belligerent, but as he tried to come up with excuses for the blood stain and the bat, Sheriff Jerry saw the fear in his eyes.

The sheriff knew he had found his main suspect.

And... that's where I'm leaving you for today's episode. We dove into the search for Darcy Cantrell and the various leads that were pursued to try and uncover her whereabouts. It's a frustrating and heart-wrenching case, but we won't give up until we find the answers. Join me next time as we take a closer look at Donovan Scott. Until then, stay curious, stay safe, and keep searching for the truth.

chapter
six

DONOVAN SCOTT.

Sasha's eyes popped open in horror. She must have dreamed last night, right? Oh, please, let it have been some kind of ultra-realistic sex dream about the town's most notorious bad boy.

Though she wasn't usually prone to sex dreams, ultra-realistic or otherwise.

And she'd never had a dream that left her wet and throbbing between her legs.

And she'd never woken up to a dream holding her in thick, tattooed arms.

The demon mask he'd worn last night still sat on the nightstand, staring at her with blank eyes.

"Does the angel want to be fucked by the demon?"

Oh, God. Oh, shit.

What had she done?

Head pounding, she carefully lifted his arm from her waist and slid off the bed. She hadn't noticed last night, but the hotel room was actually a suite with a seating area in addition to the bedroom with the king-sized bed they'd thoroughly rumpled. Sliding doors divided the two spaces, and they sat open.

Where were her clothes? She needed to find them and—

She spotted her dress thrown over the couch, but when she picked it up, her heart sank. It was torn almost in two down the back along the zipper. She couldn't wear it without showing everyone her ass. She dropped it and picked her thong off a nearby lamp. It was also shredded into two pieces. If anyone saw what was left of her clothing, they'd think she'd been attacked by a feral animal rather than undressed by a man.

A man with very big, talented hands.

A man who had made her scream—

No.

She shut down the memories. She had to go home and forget this ever happened, but she couldn't very well creep out of here naked.

The black shirt he'd been wearing last night lay in a heap on the floor. It didn't suit him. She knew from seeing him around Redwood Coast Rescue that he was a leather jacket and jeans kind of guy. Zak must have blackmailed him to get him to dress up in costume for the ball.

Well, it was better than nothing. She grabbed it and pulled the shirt over her head. It hung on her, skimming her thighs. The satin was cool against her skin, making her nipples pucker, and the deep V neckline showed off more cleavage than her dress had. She tried to lace the string tighter, closing the gap. It was no use.

It wasn't often she felt petite, but Donovan was a big man with broad, powerful shoulders. She remembered the way he'd picked her up like—

No, dammit.

"Where are you going?"

She jumped at the rumble of his sleep-roughened voice

behind her and clutched the V-neck closed as she spun toward him. He was still wearing nothing but his tattoos, and he was hard, his morning erection jutting shamelessly. The man was all diamond-cut muscle, his broad shoulders narrowing into a defined V at his hips. Every inch of him was perfect, which made her feel even more self-conscious. She was strong—she had to be to treat horse-sized dogs, vicious chihuahuas, and angry cats—but her muscle was hidden under a comfortable layer of fat she couldn't get rid of no matter how much she exercised and dieted. She was soft and round in all the places he was hard and flat. She held the gaping neck of the shirt tighter and tugged on the too-short hem.

He leaned a shoulder against the doorframe as his gaze roamed down her body. His lips quirked. "I saw all that up close last night, angel. No sense in covering up now."

Her headache roared back, reminding her exactly how much champagne she'd drunk. "I need to go home, but *you* ripped my dress."

"You were taking too long getting out of it."

"Oh my God." Heat burned her cheeks. She was probably tomato-red. She turned away and gathered what was left of her clothes. "Last night was such a mistake. What was I thinking?"

"Showing up in that dress, you were thinking you wanted to get laid. And you did."

"Not by you!"

His smirk faded, and a dark shutter fell over his features. He pushed away from the wall and prowled toward her. "Then by who?"

She refused to feel bad. She'd just been telling the truth, after all. "It's not important."

"It is to me." He backed her against the wall and caged her in with a palm planted on each side of her head. "Who were you trying to seduce?"

She tilted her chin up and kept her lips pressed firmly

together, but she didn't need to answer. She saw the moment he connected the dots. Something vulnerable flickered in his eyes, there and gone in a blink, then his lip curled in disgust.

"Ash. Of course."

Okay, dammit, she did feel bad. "I'm sorry. You're just not—"

"What? Civilized?"

"My type."

"Angel, with the way you screamed last night, I'm *exactly* your type."

"I was drunk."

"No, you weren't. Tipsy, maybe, but I wouldn't have taken you if you were drunk."

"Well, there's a difference between sexual compatibility and—"

He gripped her chin in his hand and stared down into her eyes. "You think you want the sheriff, but he's too good. You'd be bored of him within a month because he'll never make you as wet as I can. Are you on birth control?"

God, she felt like she was on a tilt-o-whirl with this man. Her head was spinning. "What?"

"It's an easy question. Are. You. On. Birth control?"

"Uh... yes."

"Good." His mouth dropped to hover over hers as his free hand dipped between her legs. "Because we're out of condoms, and you're not leaving here without my handprint on your ass and my cum leaking down your leg."

chapter
seven

IT WAS the wrong thing to say. Donovan knew it as soon as the words left his lips.

Anger flashed in her eyes. "You can't talk to me like that."

"You liked it last night."

"That was last night." She shoved a hand against his chest. "Now back off."

He held up his hands, took a step back, and told himself the rejection didn't hurt. His dirty mouth hadn't bothered her when he was her demon. He'd worn that stupid mask, and she'd been able to convince herself he was someone else. But now, in the harsh light of dawn, she couldn't deny his identity anymore, and she was disgusted.

Had he really thought this would go any differently?

Chin lifted like a queen staring down at a peasant not worth her time, she stepped past him. "I'm leaving."

Sasha grabbed her tattered dress and stepped into it. A pity. He liked the way she looked in his shirt and the way the hem rode up just enough to give the occasional tantalizing peek at the lush globes of her ass. The dress was obviously ripped, but the shirt was long enough to keep her from indecent exposure. She walked to the door.

Fuck. Donovan exhaled hard and rubbed his hands over his head. This woman had starred in all his X-rated fantasies for over a year—ever since he first saw her at Redwood Coast Rescue—and now she was walking away.

He couldn't let her leave like this, with indignation snapping in her eyes. Especially if this was the only night they were going to have together. He didn't want the beauty of it to be soured by regret.

"Hey, Sasha, wait."

She paused with her hand on the doorknob. "What?"

"Do you have a ride?"

She was silent for a beat. "Zak was my ride."

"I'm sure he's gone home by now."

"It's fine. I'll figure something out."

"I can drive you home. Just give me a minute to dress." He went to the bedroom and grabbed fresh clothes out of his bag.

"My car's at the rescue," she called after him.

"Then I'll drive you there." He pulled on jeans and a sweatshirt and then hesitated a beat, staring at the rumpled bed. Goddammit. This was not how he'd wanted the night to end. He shouldered his bag and returned to the living room to find Sasha still standing by the door, her arms wrapped around herself as if she was cold.

"You don't have to—"

He waved aside her protest as he stuffed his feet into his boots. "Nah, it's fine. I'm heading that way anyway. I have to pick up Spirit from the kennel."

At the mention of his dog, some of the tension eased out of her spine. "How is she?"

Okay, if she was more comfortable talking dogs, then he could talk dogs. Luckily, Spirit was one of his favorite topics. He opened the door and waited for her to go out ahead of him. He took the Do Not Disturb hanger off the knob and tossed it into the room before shutting the door.

Sasha stood in the hallway, self-consciously plucking at the deep-V collar of his costume shirt. He could've offered her another shirt from his bag, but he liked the view. And if this car ride was all the time he had left with her, he was going to be a selfish bastard and enjoy it.

"Spirit's perfect," he replied and started toward the elevator. "It's like she never had that tumor. She loves agility and aced her explosives detection training. We finished the twelve-week course a few days ago, and we're just waiting on the certification paperwork to go through."

A smile softened her expression as she fell into step next to him. "I'm relieved to hear that. I was so nervous during that entire surgery. Poking around the brain like that is always scary."

He stopped abruptly, and she nearly walked into him. She peeked around him as if expecting to see someone they knew up ahead.

The hall was empty.

She released her breath in a whoosh, then her brows wrinkled with confusion. "What's wrong?"

He faced her. "*You* did Spirit's surgery?"

"Um..." Her gaze bounced around like she wasn't sure how to answer and was looking for an out. "Yes?"

He didn't know why that hadn't occurred to him. Of course she had done the surgery. She was the rescue's vet, and she'd been overseeing Spirit's recovery before he decided he wanted to be her handler. Spirit had a follow-up visit at the clinic two months ago, but Zak had taken her since he'd been in San Francisco re-certifying in explosive ordnance disposal, so he'd never talked with Sasha about her recovery before now. "You saved her life."

Now she just looked befuddled. "Uh, I don't know about saving her life. The tumor was benign. But we definitely improved the quality of her—"

"You are the most amazing woman I've ever met."

Color flooded her cheeks. "I was just doing my job, Donovan. Nothing amazing about that."

She didn't see it. Was her self-confidence really so low that she didn't know how amazing she was? "Angel, my entire life has been about destruction. I destroy everything I touch—but you? You fix. You heal. You care."

"I'm just a vet," she protested.

He shook his head, refusing to let her dismiss herself so easily. Not when he was so determined to make her see how amazing she was. He slid a hand under her chin and tilted her face up to his. "You are a hero."

Her lips parted in surprise, and she stared up at him with wide brown eyes that made his chest tighten. But then she blinked, and her expression closed down. She was determined to shut him out.

She pulled away from him and lifted her chin, her spine straightening. "We should go."

He wanted to make her see the truth. He wanted to kiss the hell out of her and then take her home—to *his* home— where he'd kiss her some more. She deserved all his kisses and anything else she wanted, as far as he was concerned.

But he stepped back. He would let her have space until she was comfortable with him again.

He followed her to the elevator and pushed the button for the parking garage. Silence stretched between them, and he was ready to do something—anything—to break it, but he didn't want to push the issue again.

The elevator doors slid open, and the scent of oil, dust, and concrete flooded in. Fluorescent bulbs flickered to life on the ceiling, revealing a large, mostly empty garage with a few cars parked at random intervals. He led her to his Jeep and suddenly, desperately wished he'd taken the time to clean it. He and Spirit had practically been living out of it while attending the K9 explosives detection training course, and the interior looked like it. He quickly stuffed several empty fast food bags into the backseat and threw Spirit's favorite blanket over them.

At least the car was relatively dirt-free, with only one muddy paw print on the dashboard.

Sasha eyed him. "Are you sure you have room in here for me?"

He stepped back, holding the door open for her. "Positive."

She smoothed her hands down the skirt of her dress, then looked up at him with a pleasant smile that seemed to be pasted on her face. Like he was a stranger she had to make small talk with and not the man who fucked her until she screamed his name mere hours ago. He shut the door and circled the hood to the driver's side. When he slid in, Sasha still had that fake, customer service smile in place.

"I'd love to hear about the explosives training. I bet it was fascinating. I've always wanted to do search and rescue with Anna, but my schedule doesn't allow for it."

He didn't want to talk about his job when it felt like it was barely one conversational step above talking about the weather —just something inane to fill the silence. She was clearly shutting him out. He'd wanted to take care of her tonight. He'd wanted to give her pleasure and protect her from the ugliness of his life. He'd wanted to make her feel special.

He shrugged. "It was training."

She glanced over at him as he started the engine. "That's it?"

"After spending your entire adult life in the military, one training's very much like the rest." Though, he had to admit, having Spirit by his side made it a more pleasant experience than most of the training he endured as a Marine.

"You did explosives in the military, too, right?"

When he raised a brow at her, she glanced down and picked at the hem of the shirt. "I heard Zak and Anna talking about it once. They said you got blown up."

Donovan returned his attention to the road. He didn't like talking about his past, but at least she'd moved beyond the fake smile and small talk. "Yeah, I did. More than once, actually."

Her eyes widened, and he could see the questions forming in her mind. He braced himself for them, knowing full well that he had to be honest with her if he wanted any shot at a second night.

"More than once?"

"I was in Iraq and Afghanistan. I was blown up by an IED in both places. The first time, it just knocked me out, gave me a concussion. But the second one...that one did some real damage." His hand tightened on the steering wheel as his chest constricted at the memory. "I lost my mind."

Her hand fluttered up to her throat and he felt her gaze trace the rope of scar tissue along his temple as surely as a caress. "You lost..."

Why was his mouth suddenly so dry? He tapped the scar. "Traumatic brain injury."

"I'm so sorry," she said softly.

He shrugged it off, trying to keep his voice steady. "It was a risk of the job. I knew what could happen when I signed up for it."

"But that doesn't make it any less painful," she said, and he could hear the pity in her voice.

No, it didn't make it any less painful. But he didn't want her to feel sorry for him. He wanted her to see him as more than his scars and his past. "It's in the past," he said firmly. "I'm here now, and I'm whole."

She turned to face him. "Are you?"

He wasn't sure if she was talking about his physical or emotional state, but he knew the answer to both. "Yes," he said. "Having Spirit with me helps. She's...she's like my anchor, you know? She keeps me grounded."

Sasha nodded slowly, her gaze fixed on him. "I could see that whenever I saw you two together at the rescue. I could see your bond. She's an amazing dog."

Donovan smiled, the tension in his chest easing slightly. "Yeah, she is."

Silence fell between them, but it felt different now. More companionable as he navigated the winding coastal road. The sky was a canvas of deep blues and purples, fading into a soft glow to the east.

But it was too early for dawn.

Sasha sucked in a sharp breath. "Is that...?"

chapter
eight

"FIRE. FUCK!" Donovan pressed the gas to the floor and burned rubber up the hill toward RWCR, jumping out of the vehicle the moment it rocked to a stop in the circular drive.

Flames engulfed the fields behind the barn and Sasha's clinic and crawled up the mountain toward the tree line. If the fire reached it, the entire town would ignite. It was moving fast, roaring as it consumed smaller trees and dry brush. Embers danced in the air, sparking more fires in the too-dry grass.

Shit, this was bad. The whole damn county hadn't seen a good rainstorm since spring.

The heat was palpable, the air thick with smoke. The acrid smell of burning wood and vegetation overwhelmed the senses, and Donovan blinked hard against the sting of it.

The fire licked toward the barn, and tendrils of smoke rose up from the back of the building as the side wall caught. The columns grew taller and thicker as he drew closer until they completely filled the sky with a gray blanket that obscured the stars.

He grabbed Sasha's shoulder, pulling her back, away from the burning building. "Go to the house! Make sure Zak,

Anna, and the girls are safe." The house was farther away from the wall of flames. She'd be safer there.

Her face was white with fear, her eyes wide and brimming with tears. "The dogs..."

"I'll get them. Do you have any overnight patients at the hospital?"

She blinked at him like she didn't understand the question.

"Sasha, focus!"

She shook off the shock. "No. No, we've been doing renovations, so I sent all of my hospitalized patients to Dr. Richards in town."

"Okay, good." The doggie daycare and hotel were closed down for the same reason, and all of the adoptable pets had been sent to either foster homes or the county SPCA until the renovations were complete. So that meant there were only two dogs in their rehab wing right now: the scarred Golden Retriever, Matilda, and the newest resident, a black German Shepherd named Dante, a state police K9 who had been wounded on the job when his handler was killed. And, of course, Spirit. He'd left her here in her old kennel since he'd planned to be gone all night.

Jesus. Spirit was in there. His heart jumped into his throat as he turned toward the building.

Sasha grabbed his hand. "Be careful."

He gave her fingers a quick squeeze. "I will. Go wake Zak and Anna." It was weird they weren't already awake and trying to save the dogs themselves, but he couldn't worry about them right now.

He had to get to Spirit.

He raced toward the barn's front door, but intense heat pushed him back. Ashes rained down on his head like snow. The fire was deafening now, a crackling roar that blocked out all other sounds. He circled the building, searching for another way in, but the flames licked at every window and doorway.

Finally, a small window caught his eye. Its glass was shattered and blackened from the fire, but there were no flames dancing beyond it. Without hesitation, Donovan sprinted towards it and hurled himself through the jagged opening, slicing open his arm on the glass. He was in the conference room where he attended group therapy every week. The smoke hit him like a physical blow, threatening to overwhelm him, but he gritted his teeth and pressed on through the lobby to C-wing, where all the dogs who needed a bit of extra love were housed.

The entire backside of the building was engulfed now, and the roof creaked ominously overhead. As he approached the kennels, a sense of dread filled him. What if he was too late? What if—

But then he saw a flash of gold fur in the first kennel. Matilda. The poor dog had already been badly burned once before and was tucked into the corner, pressed against the wall, her high whine barely audible above the fire. This was going to set her rehabilitation back by months.

He grabbed a leash and opened the kennel, but Matilda wouldn't move. He gave up on the leash, picked her up, and draped her over his shoulders.

Dante, in the next kennel, was growling, his dark fur standing straight up along his spine. Shit. He'd need the muzzle, but he didn't have time to wrestle it on the dog.

Spirit stood in the middle of her kennel, eerily silent. She was usually a vocal dog. He opened her kennel and called her, but she didn't move. Her tailed tucked between her legs, and she crouched low, flattening her ears to her head.

On his shoulders, Matilda started to struggle, her claws ripping into his shirt and skin.

He couldn't get them all out.

"Van!"

Relief crashed through him at the sound of another human voice. He didn't even care that it was Ash fucking Rawlings.

"Van, where are you?"

"C-wing!" he called back, then coughed hard as smoke filled his lungs.

Ash appeared in the doorway, covered in soot, backlit by an orange glow. "Let's go! We're going to lose the barn."

"Get Dante. I'll take Matilda out and come back for Spirit."

"There isn't—"

But Donovan didn't hear the rest. He sprinted out the back door into the agility yard. The fire was close. Too close.

"Sasha!"

She stood out in the driveway, the fire dancing orange over her horrified face as she watched her vet clinic ignite, but she turned toward him at the sound of her name. He heaved Matilda up over the fence. "Get her in the Jeep. Get out of here!"

"Wait—"

He couldn't. He turned and ran back toward the barn. He passed Ash coming out with Dante over his shoulders. The shepherd wasn't wearing a muzzle, but he wasn't growling either. Whatever Ash had done to win his trust worked.

Ash tried to catch his arm. "Van, don't—"

He shook off the grip and plunged into the barn. The heat was intense now and scorched his face. The smoke had grown so thick that it felt like he was breathing in a hot blanket, but he had to keep moving. If he stopped, the flames would swallow him whole, and Spirit would die. He could hear them crackling around him as he forced himself to keep going despite the fear that was urging him to turn back. His courage had kept him alive as a boy, and he drew on every ounce of it now.

The sound of Spirit's frightened whimpers guided him through the dense, black smoke. His eyes streamed with tears. His skin blistered. His lungs screaming for fresh air, but he wouldn't abandon his girl.

If they were going to die like this, they would be together.

Through the haze, he saw Spirit's small form huddled in the far corner of the C-wing hallway, her fur singed and her eyes wide with terror. She had left her kennel after all but hadn't known which way to go and instead ran toward the fire. Now she was trapped.

He took a step toward her—

And the ceiling crumbled on top of him.

Pain lanced through his skull, as bright as the fire, and his vision swam with black spots. His jaw throbbed as if someone had punched him in the face, and then he realized that, yeah, something had. The floor. He staggered to his feet and reached through the flames for Spirit's collar. Her fur was hot, and she bared her teeth at him like he was the one causing her pain.

"Hey, sweetheart. It's okay. I'm here now."

She whimpered and inched toward him, tentatively licking his hand. He pulled her into his chest, trying to shield her from the heat. "Shh, I'm here. I'm here with you."

His mind fogged, and his limbs grew heavy. He'd lost consciousness enough times to know he was losing the battle to stay awake. But with the fire at their backs and death heavy in the air around them, if he closed his eyes now, that would be the end of Donovan Scott.

No more fighting with his scrambled brain.

No more group therapy sessions that prodded at all his old wounds until he bled.

Wood popped and crackled and groaned around them as the fire chewed through more of the structure.

No more fucking podcasts digging into his life.

The air dried out in his lungs, making it hard to breathe.

No more training with Spirit.

No more nights with Sasha.

He forced his eyes open. No. He wasn't going out like this.

He staggered to his feet, and pieces of the ceiling fell off his back. At least none of the debris was on fire. He turned his back to the flames and pushed slowly down the hall, shielding Spirit with his body. His throat was raw, and his skin felt like it was being flayed from his bones. His vision kept clouding over, and he couldn't think straight anymore. All he could do was move. One foot in front of the other.

He had to get to the other end of the hall. He had to get outside.

The floor cracked beneath his feet, and flames kissed his ankles. He stumbled, then caught himself and started moving again. He could see the outline of the door through the smoke. All he had to do was get through it. Just a few more feet...

Something wet nudged his arm. He looked down at his girl. Spirit was struggling to keep her eyes open. When she gazed up at him with such love and trust, it felt like a punch to his gut. His tears evaporated off his face as they fell. Fire caught his sleeve, and he batted at it. The hallway tilted and he crashed into the wall.

From the corner of his eye, he saw a flash of yellow—another person?

He tried to call out to them, but the smoke strangled him. The figure just stood there with the flames reflected in its dark bug eyes, watching. It was grinning. He couldn't see its mouth under the—mask? Was it wearing a respirator? But he knew it was smiling at him, enjoying his struggle.

No, it couldn't be a real person. Nobody but him would be crazy enough to run into this fire. He was hallucinating, losing what was left of his fractured mind. He fought against the blackness that was dragging him under, no longer certain which way was up.

And Spirit had gone limp in his arms. He staggered and dropped to one knee. The door was too far away.

The fire was winning.

No!

With a burst of desperate adrenaline, he shoved to his feet and hurled himself through the door. The grass outside was wet and felt amazing on his burning skin. He lay there for a moment, head spinning as he sucked in lungfuls of air. It was still laced with smoke, but it was cleaner than what he had been breathing inside.

Pain pierced his side with each shallow inhale. He touched his ribs gingerly and felt a sticky warmth there. He winced. He didn't know how bad it was but suspected he needed urgent medical attention sooner rather than later.

And Spirit still hadn't moved.

Desperation clawed at his throat as he again tried to call out for help, but his voice was nothing more than a wheeze. He heard voices. Figures filled his hazy vision. Sirens echoed off the mountains in the distance, and hope fluttered within him as he closed his eyes.

He could let go now.

Help was on its way.

He drifted, caught somewhere between consciousness and sleep, and thought of Sasha. The way she'd felt under him in bed. The horror in her eyes when he finally took off that damn demon mask and she realized who she'd spent the night with. Her reaction had hurt, but he should've expected nothing less. He was the town pariah, after all. The delinquent from the way wrong side of the tracks. The suspected killer.

Forget that he'd lost all but the thinnest shred of sanity serving his country. Forget that he had poured his heart and soul into Redwood Coast Rescue since Zak handed him Spirit's leash and recruited him to the new tactical K9 team.

This fucking town couldn't let go of the troublemaking kid he'd been.

As the ambulance arrived and the paramedics rushed to his side, he heard a voice in the distance. A woman's voice. He liked the sound of her saying his name.

"Donovan, can you hear me?" someone was asking him. Not the woman. He wanted her voice back. "We need to get you to the hospital. You've been badly burned."

He nodded, but his head felt weirdly floaty like it wasn't connected to his body. He drifted again. Opened his eyes sometime later to see the sterile white ceiling of an ambulance. Spirit was still nestled against his chest, licking his cheek. Her warmth and weight were a comfort.

And the woman's voice was back, alternately soothing and snapping out orders. That was a comfort, too.

He closed his eyes again, feeling his heart rate slow as he floated away. In his dreams, he saw the figure in the flames staring at him. It wasn't human. It was an omen, something ominous looming on the horizon...

Something that was going to change everything.

episode 3: the main suspect

Hey, Truth Seekers! Welcome back to Cold Truth, the true-crime podcast where we dig deep into cold cases and, hopefully, find new leads. I'm your host, Alexis Summers, and in today's episode, we're going to talk about Donovan Scott, the main suspect in Darcy's disappearance, and his suspicious past.

So, you won't believe this, but about six months before Darcy vanished, Donovan was actually the prime suspect in another death. But before we get to that, we need to go back in time to understand exactly who Darcy's boyfriend was.

Donovan Kevin Scott was born on June 11, 1990, to Ellen and Rueben "Rooster" Scott. His parents were high school sweethearts from San Francisco and got married at age seventeen when Ellen discovered she was pregnant. Rooster dropped out of school and worked as a dock hand while Ellen finished out her senior year, graduating mere days before they welcomed their son. Unfortunately, neither came from supportive families and since they couldn't afford childcare, they made the decision to have Ellen stay home, which strained their relationship and finances even further. The city was too expensive and getting more expensive every year.

They needed to move.

Just as Donovan was about to enter elementary school, Rooster was offered a position on a crabbing boat up north. It seemed like the fresh start that the young family needed. They settled into a trailer park outside the scenic town of Steam Valley and quickly made friends with the family next door: the Cantrells.

From that day on, Donovan Scott and Darcy Cantrell were inseparable.

Like Darcy, Donovan was searching for a way out. Unlike Darcy, he decided early on that school was his ticket to freedom—specifically school athletics. He had enough raw talent for baseball that by his freshmen year of high school, college recruiters were already sniffing around. But with high school came trouble. Donovan couldn't seem to stay out of it, and the recruiters moved on to less risky candidates.

As the kids grew, both of their homes became more volatile. Rooster started drinking heavily and quit his crabbing job to open his own recreational fishing charter. Money was beyond tight because Rooster spent every penny he made at the town bars. Ellen worked full-time at a nearby truck stop and cleaned houses on the side to try and make ends meet.

In the eight-year period between the Scotts' move to Steam Valley and Donovan hitting puberty, records show he and Ellen visited the hospital an astounding total of one-hundred-and-fifty-three times for various injuries. That's nearly *ten visits* per year for each of them.

A broken arm— "He fell out of a tree."

A black eye— "I slipped in the shower."

A knocked-out tooth— "He crashed his bike."

Cracked ribs— "I tripped while taking out the garbage."

Everyone knew what was really happening behind the closed door of their trailer, but like Sissy Cantrell, Ellen never pressed charges against her husband for the abuse. And like

Darcy, Donovan never mentioned it to anyone—not even his closest friends, Zak Hendricks and Ash Rawlings, knew how bad it was.

But Darcy knew.

She wrote about Donovan extensively in her diary, which was "accidentally" leaked to the public during the investigation. Little of what she wrote was flattering, especially in the last few turbulent months before she vanished.

Here's an excerpt from Darcy's diary entry from April 9th, 2007:

> "Van finally won a fight. He knocked Rooster flat-out with his baseball bat. If Rooster ever puts another bruise on his mom, he said he'd kill the fucker. He loves Ellen so much. I wonder if he'd do the same for me if I asked him. I'd give him the bat and watch him bash Dad's head in, and wouldn't feel anything. But I don't think he loves me that much. Sometimes, I think he'd rather bash MY head in."

Ominous, right?

Well, it gets worse.

Weeks later, Rooster's boat was found floating off-shore, empty but still running. His body washed up on the beach at Lost Rocks State Park the following day.

Cause of death?

Blunt force trauma to the head.

It had people talking, and even Darcy wondered in her diary if Donovan had made good on his threat.

However, an autopsy showed Rooster's blood-alcohol

level was more than four times the legal limit—a level that would be almost fatal for most people—and the medical examiner ultimately listed the manner of death as accidental. The consensus by investigators at the time was Rooster had taken his boat out while drunk and fell overboard, where he was thrown against the rocks by stormy seas.

Case closed.

But ask anyone in town what happened to Rooster Scott, and you'll get the same answer: Donovan killed him.

Now, fast forward to Darcy's disappearance, and it seems like Donovan might be the main suspect again. But we'll get to the reasons for that in the next episode, where we'll continue our investigation. Thanks for listening, and don't forget to subscribe for more true crime stories. And as always, stay curious, stay safe, and keep seeking the truth. See you next time!

chapter
nine

THREE DAYS.

Donovan had been unconscious for three whole days and counting.

Sasha stayed at his bedside, leaving only when the nurses kicked her out at night. Then she went home and paced and worried until she could go back the next morning. She took comfort in the fact that his doctors hadn't seen the need to transfer him to a bigger trauma hospital.

On the afternoon of the third day, Zak and Anna stopped by. They both looked exhausted, but their concern for her when they stepped into the room was palpable. What did that say about how she looked?

"Hey, Sash," Anna said gently and squeezed her shoulder. "When was the last time you ate?"

When she didn't answer right away—because she honestly couldn't remember—Anna pulled on her hand. "C'mon. Let's go get some fries."

"Oh. I don't know—"

"Zak will stay with him." She sent a meaningful look at her husband, and Zak nodded.

"Yeah, I'll hang out and chat with him."

Still, she hesitated. "What if—"

"If he wakes up," Zak added, "you'll be the first to know. Go on."

Down in the cafeteria, Sasha picked a salad over fries but regretted it instantly. The lettuce was wilted, and there was only one sad cherry tomato on top. She poked at it with her fork. Maybe if she doused it in ranch dressing, it wouldn't be so bad. "Is the fire still burning?"

Anna took a sip of her milkshake and sat back in her seat with a heavy sigh. "Yeah. The whole mountain is on fire. They estimate it's at fourteen thousand acres now and still growing, but it's burning east, so they don't think the town is in danger. At least not yet. I hate that this fire carries my family's name. The Double R Fire. For Rawlings Ranch. Zak says it's because they're named for where they're first reported, but it sucks. Why couldn't they have called it... I don't know... the Hella Hot Fire or the Smokin' Squirrels Scorch? Honestly, anything would be better than slapping my family's name on it."

Anna often rambled when she was upset, and she had every right in the world to her anger and sadness right now, so Sasha just rolled with it. "What about The Humboldt Heatwave?"

"Oh, that's a good one. The Trinity Toaster."

"The Shasta Sizzler?"

"That sounds like a burger." Her lower lip trembled, and tears spilled over. "Oh. My kitchen. I'll never make dinner there again. I loved my kitchen."

Sasha's heart ached for her best friend. She'd lost the clinic she'd spent her whole life working toward, and it felt like she'd lost a limb. She couldn't even imagine how it must feel to lose everything you owned. "I know, sweetie. I'm so sorry. Is anything salvageable?"

"No." Anna pulled her straw out of her milkshake and jabbed it back in. "It's all gone. The barn, your clinic, my parents' house. All of my pictures. Our daughter's grave...." Her voice cracked, and she trailed off.

Sasha reached for her hand. "Are you okay?"

Anna sniffled and swiped at her eyes with the backs of her hands. "I don't know. I was considering selling the land to Monarch—"

"No, you can't! It's all insured, and we'll rebuild, bigger and better than before. It's not like we didn't need new facilities anyway. That's why we were renovating in the first place. Now we'll be able to build to our exact specifications. We can make my clinic bigger, expand the training facility, and give Zak's team their own space."

Anna sighed. "Logically, I know all of that. But the amount of work it'll take... it's daunting. And what about you? You can't go months without working while we rebuild. You'll lose all your patients."

"Don't worry about me. Dr. Richards said I could work out of his practice in town until I have my own clinic again. He's cut way back on his hours in preparation for retirement and never hired another vet after I left, so my old office is even still available. It'll be okay." She squeezed Anna's hand. "We'll get through this. You don't have to sell."

"I know. And I wouldn't. I don't know why I even said that. This land has been in my family since the Gold Rush, and I'm not giving it to some corporation to develop into hotels and condos that will price people out of town. I just spiraled for a couple of days, but then Zak reminded me this morning that we didn't lose everything. We still have Bella and Poppy and both of our dogs. We're so lucky they were at his parents' house that night. And we're lucky we decided to stay there after the fundraiser instead of going home. We could've slept right through it, and then we would've orphaned the girls again."

A chill scraped down Sasha's spine. "Oh, don't say that."

"But it's true. We were *so* lucky. And we're lucky that Zak's brother digitized the pictures of our daughter, so we at least still have those. We're even lucky that we've been doing those damn renovations, so we didn't have a full house at the rescue. And, thanks to Donovan, the dogs that were there are safe."

Now Sasha's eyes flooded with tears. "He ran in there without a second thought to his own safety. He was so determined to get to Spirit and the others. It was incredibly brave."

Anna scowled. "And incredibly stupid."

"Would you rather he not have gone in for the dogs?" Wow, where had that surge of defensive protectiveness come from? Anna was right. It had been stupid and risky. She even had the exact same thought as she paced in front of the barn and watched it burn with Donovan inside. She'd cursed him and feared for him and told herself if he lived through it, she'd never sleep with him again. She didn't need his kind of danger in her life.

So why did she feel the need to defend him now?

"No, of course not," Anna sighed. "I'm glad he saved them. But, still, it scared Zak. He won't admit it, but he loves the guy, you know? He's pissed that Donovan took the risk without backup."

"Really? He didn't look mad."

Anna released a soft huff of laughter. "He gets angry when he's scared, and I'm sure he's bitching Donovan out right now. But it's fine. He'll get over it when Donovan wakes up."

The knot of dread that had been tying up Sasha's stomach for the last three days tightened painfully. She pushed her salad aside. "*If* he wakes up."

"He will." Anna said it with absolute certainty and waved a hand, dismissing the idea that he wouldn't. Then she deftly changed the subject: "How are the dogs? I haven't had a chance to go to Dr. Richards' and check on them."

Did best friends get any better than Anna? Sasha seriously doubted it, because nobody else could've known she desperately needed the subject change. "They're good. They all have burns, but nothing life-threatening. Spirit definitely got the worst of it, plus smoke inhalation, but she's already healing."

Better and faster than her owner.

Dammit, why wouldn't he wake up?

She cleared her throat and forced her wandering thoughts back to the dogs: "Uh, Dante's been a bit of a problem. He's still in guard mode, not letting anyone close to his kennel. And, unfortunately, Matilda is back to cowering in the corner of her kennel."

Anna groaned. "Dammit. All that work we've done with her..." She snapped her fingers. "Gone. I've really loved seeing her come out of her shell, and now she's going to retreat even farther into it."

"She'll bounce back," Sasha said, trying to inject as much certainty into her voice as Anna had about Donovan waking up. "She's already proven she's strong and resilient."

"Yeah, it'll just take a lot of work. And now I'll have to disrupt her more and find a new place for her to live while we rebuild—"

"I'll take her." The words surprised Sasha even as they popped out of her mouth. She hadn't had a pet since her four-teen-year-old black lab passed away from cancer last year, and she hadn't planned on getting another one any time soon. But this felt right.

Anna looked at her, stunned. "You sure you're ready for another pet? I thought you were still grieving for Roscoe."

She nodded. "I'll always grieve. He was my boy, and I miss him every day, but I think it's time."

Anna's eyes welled up again. "Thank you so much. That's such a relief. One less thing I have to worry about. Now I'll just have to find someone who can handle Hurricane Dante."

"Give him to Ash."

Anna nearly choked on a sip of her milkshake. "Oh, yeah, he'd love that. I can hear him now..." She deepened her voice, mimicking her twin: "'I don't have time for one of your lost causes, AJ.'"

"He'll take him, though, if you ask. He'll do anything for you."

"Yes, I know he would, but he has a lot going on with this fire. I can't ask him to take Dante on, too. Not now, at least."

They sat in silence for a few moments, both lost in their own thoughts. Tears dripped down Anna's cheeks again, and Sasha was at a loss of what to say to comfort her.

"Okay, enough sad talk." Anna swiped away her tears with both hands, then leaned forward conspiratorially. "Time to spill the tea. You and Donovan? Um, excuse me, ma'am, when did that happen? Was it at the fundraiser? And what about Ash?"

Sasha groaned inwardly. She'd expected the questions but had hoped recent events would put them off for a bit longer. Especially since she still wasn't sure how she felt about the whole Donovan thing. It was easier to focus on his injuries than what came before and what could potentially happen after. "It... didn't happen."

"Sash, you were wearing the man's shirt that morning over your *ripped dress*. Don't you try to tell me it didn't happen. C'mon, I thought we were friends!"

"Okay, okay." Sasha laughed. "Don't give me those puppy eyes. I can't take it."

Anna batted her lashes. "Then spill."

"I mean, yeah. It happened, and it was..." She couldn't even find words for it and made an exploding motion by her temples.

Anna smirked. "Yeah, I bet it was."

"But we're not a couple. It was a semi-drunken one-night thing."

"Says the woman who has sat at his bedside for three days."

"What, I'm not allowed to be worried?" Her hands clenched on the table as she replayed images that she feared would be etched in her mind forever – a wall of flames devouring the mountain, a lone figure walking out of the barn with a dog in his arms, engulfed in smoke and fire, his jacket disintegrating as he emerged. "I watched him walk out of a flaming building while *on fire*. His jacket *melted*."

Anna's eyes softened. "Of course you're allowed to worry."

"If it were you or Zak or Ash or any of our friends, I'd still be here."

"Okay." Anna held up her hands. "Sorry. I didn't mean anything by it."

Sasha closed her eyes and took a moment to rein in the unexpected surge of defensiveness. "No, I'm the one who should be apologizing. I'm sorry I snapped. I'm tired."

Anna reached across the table and gave her hand a comforting squeeze. "We all are, honey."

"There is something between Donovan and me," she admitted with a sigh. "I just... don't know how to classify it. And until he wakes up and we can figure it out, I'd rather not discuss it."

"Okay, fair." Anna pressed her lips together and made it all of two heartbeats before blurting, "But Donovan? I know he's hot as hell, but... I mean... you know the rumors about him."

"I'm aware." Everybody in town knew the rumors, and everybody in town had their theories. Until the other night, she'd never really had an opinion about it. While Donovan and Darcy were in her graduating class, she'd only known them in passing. And at the time of Darcy's disappearance, she'd been too wrapped up in her own trauma to care.

But now?

A man who would risk his life to save three dogs couldn't also be a cold-blooded killer. Of that, she was certain.

"And what about Ash?" Anna asked. "You finally caught his eye at the fundraiser. I know he's planning on taking you to dinner when things calm down around here."

A sharp pang of guilt twisted in Sasha's chest. "Ash is great, but he's not..." She searched for the right words. He was not... what? Donovan? Well, obviously. They were two very different men. One was by the book and the other had burned the book a long time ago. "I don't want you to think I'm leading your brother on. I'm not. When things settle down, I'll tell him. It's just... Donovan... he makes me..."

"Feel?" Anna suggested.

"Yes," she breathed. "All the things."

Anna nodded slowly. "I get it. It was the same for me when Zak came back into my life, despite all the warning bells telling me I shouldn't get involved with him again."

"But that turned out okay."

"Yes, it did. After a lot of drama and other stuff. But Donovan... in a lot of ways, he has more baggage than even Zak."

Sasha snorted a laugh. "Nobody has more baggage than Zak Hendricks."

"Well, maybe that was true a couple years ago, but now, he's in a better headspace than me most days. The point is, I just don't want you to get hurt."

"I appreciate that, but I know what I'm doing." She hoped. "I can take care of myself."

Anna grinned. "Damn right, you can. That's one of the many reasons I love you."

Sasha smiled back, grateful for the subject change. "Love

you too, Anna. And thank you, again, for letting me take Matilda. I'll pick her up on my way home tonight."

"I couldn't think of anyone better for her, Sash. And hey, like you said, we'll rebuild. We'll come back stronger and better than ever."

Sasha nodded but couldn't shake the feeling that things would never be the same. The fire had destroyed everything, and yet it seemed to have ignited something within her. The feelings she had for Donovan were more than just physical attraction that she could ignore. She cared about him in a way that she couldn't explain. But did he feel the same way?

But for now, all she could do was sit and wait by Donovan's bedside, hoping he would wake up soon.

When Zak and Anna left, she reached out and took his hand again. She traced the lines of his palm, wondering what he was dreaming about, and his fingers twitched beneath hers. She gasped, staring down at his hand. His fingers twitched again. She leaned in closer, watching as his eyelids fluttered.

Donovan's eyes slowly opened, and he blinked a few times. His lips parted, and a small groan escaped him.

"Donovan?" she whispered.

His gaze fastened on her, and for a moment, he seemed to struggle to remember who she was. But then, his eyes widened with recognition, and he smiled weakly. He tried to speak, but no sound came out, and he coughed, wincing in pain.

Sasha reached for the glass of water on the table, holding it to his lips, helping him drink. Relief flooded her and brought a rush of tears to her eyes. "You're okay. You're okay now." She leaned down and pressed her lips against his cheek, the rough stubble of his three-day beard scraping against her skin. "God, you scared me."

"Sasha..." His voice was nothing more than a gravelly rasp of sound. "What happened?"

"The fire," she said softly. "You saved the dogs."

"Fire?" His brow furrowed as if he couldn't remember. "Is everyone okay?"

She nodded. "They're all being taken care of. But you—you have some serious burns."

He looked down at his bandaged arms and winced. "Yeah, I remember now." He groaned as he tried to sit up.

She quickly stood and placed her hand on his chest, urging him to stay still. "No, don't move."

He looked at her, his gaze intense. "How long have I been out?"

"You were more than just *out*. You were in a coma for three days. The barn's ceiling collapsed when you were still inside, and you have a bad concussion."

"Great," he muttered. "More scrambled eggs."

"What?"

He shut his eyes. "Nothing. Just explains why I'm seeing two of you."

"Only two?"

"Yeah, I think so. But..." He squinted at her, then his eyes shifted to the corner of the room. He stared like he saw something there. She looked over her shoulder, a chill racing down her spine. The corner was empty.

Her stomach twisted with dread. He'd already suffered a major brain injury. What if this knock on the head had done more irreparable damage? "You just need some more rest. Let me get the nurse to check on you."

He caught her hand before she could turn away. "Is Ash here? I need to talk to him."

"I think he was a little bit ago. I'll go see if he's still here and get a nurse." She stood and walked out of the room, closing the door behind her. As she approached the nurse's station, she heard someone call her name. Turning around, she saw Ash at the other end of the hallway by the elevators.

"Sasha," he said, concern heavy in his tone, "is everything okay?"

She nodded. "Donovan woke up. He's asking for you."

His expression darkened at the mention of Donovan's name. "Of course he is. But I meant *you*." He reached for her hand and gently squeezed. "Are you okay?"

"I'm fine." Guilt twinged. "But, uh, Ash? I actually need to talk to you about something..."

"I'm sorry, can it wait?" he asked, his gaze locked on Donovan's room. Tension radiated off him. He was in work mode, and the anxiety that had been tickling at the back of her brain for days changed to an icy fear.

She glanced from him to the door and back. "What's going on?"

Ash's gaze stayed on the door. "I don't trust him. He's always been trouble."

"I know he has a past, but he saved the dogs, Ash. He's in the hospital because he risked his life to protect them. Not many other men would do that."

He exhaled hard and finally looked away from the door. He tried to gentle his expression, but he was still all pissed-off cop. "Listen, I know it seems like he's a good guy under all that swagger, but I've known him a long time. He's bad news, Sash. Please, just do me a favor and stay away from him."

Her stomach twisted at the intensity in his voice. She had known he didn't like Donovan, but she hadn't realized how deeply he felt about it. "Didn't you used to be friends? What happened between you two?"

"Ask him."

"I'm asking you."

He clenched his jaw. "It's not important. What's important is that you stay away from him. He'll only hurt you in the end."

"I don't believe that. Donovan has been nothing but kind to me."

"That's because he wants something from you," Ash spat out, his eyes flashing with anger. "He's not a good guy, Sasha."

"Why are you saying this now? What happened?"

A nurse walked by right then and disappeared into Donovan's room. Ash took her by the arm and led her over to the elevator. He lowered his voice. "Listen, I shouldn't be telling you this, but I need you to be safe. Okay? So if I tell you this, you'll stay away from Donovan and let me do my job without worrying about you?"

She hesitated a beat, then nodded. "Okay."

He took a breath and let it out in a slow exhale. "Okay. A group of hotshots fighting the fire uncovered a body on the mountain. It's badly burned, and there's no telling if we'll get any DNA, but we strongly suspect it's Darcy Cantrell."

"Oh my God." She lifted a trembling hand to her mouth. "You found her?"

chapter
ten

AS SASHA STEPPED out into the hall, Donovan closed his eyes and let the world slip out of focus. The pressure in his head was intense, and he saw it pounding with each pulse of blood behind his eyes. He sank back into the flattened pillows propped behind him, but that didn't help. A wave of dizziness washed over him, and his stomach lurched.

Fuck. He was not going to be sick in front of Sasha.

He swallowed back the surge of bile and turned his gaze toward the door, careful not to move his head or look at the corner of the room.

Where was Sasha? She still hadn't returned.

"She's not coming back," the hallucination said.

Jesus fucking Christ. He had to get a grip. "You're not really there."

In the months after his TBI, he'd had night terrors that seeped into his waking hours. Visions so real, he'd once attacked a guy in a bar because he thought the man was a terrorist wearing a bomb vest. He thought he was past it—it had been a long time since his last hallucination—but apparently, this concussion had triggered them again.

Darcy Cantrell was *not* standing in the corner of his hospital room. She'd been gone for a very long time.

Vanished.

Dead.

He took deep, even breaths, just like his therapist had taught him. But the more he tried to control his breathing, the more he felt himself slipping into a panic attack. Sweat beaded on his forehead, and his heart raced, banging around in the too-small confines of his chest. His fingers dug into the sheets by his hips.

"That won't work, Van. It never works." Darcy's ghost scoffed as she moved into his line of sight. She looked exactly the same as the last time he saw her: dark hair up in a ponytail with her bangs swept to the side, big hoop earrings sparkling at her ears, a short gray denim vest over a black shirt, and a thick, studded black belt circling her hips. As always, when she appeared to him, she only wore one of her red canvas shoes. Her other foot was bare. "You can't breathe me away. You'll never get rid of me."

"You're not real. You're just a figment of my fucked up brain. Not real. Not real." Eyes squeezed shut, he repeated it to himself, over and over, until his breathing slowly returned to normal. He opened his eyes once again and scanned the room, taking note of every little detail in an attempt to ground himself in reality. The bland gray walls, the beeping machines, the sterile smell of disinfectant in the too-cold air.

And Darcy wasn't here.

The sheets—too starched and white. The blanket—too thin and scratchy. The hospital gown—too stiff and rough against his raw, burned skin. The tape holding the IV in his hand itched.

And Darcy. Wasn't. Here.

But Sasha should be. Where the hell was she?

A figure appeared in the doorway, long hair in a ponytail.

The panic surged back, and he opened his mouth to scream at her—

No, not Darcy.

Just a nurse. He snapped his mouth shut and told himself to fucking relax. He'd gotten through this once. He could do it again.

The nurse took his vitals and made a big fuss over the fact he was awake, like popping his eyes open was an Olympic sport and he'd just won gold. He tolerated her poking and prodding with barely-restrained impatience.

Fuck, he hated hospitals.

When she finally left with the promise of bringing back a doctor, another figure stepped through the door.

But it wasn't Darcy again.

And it wasn't Sasha, either.

Ash.

Right. He had asked to see the guy but couldn't help the bitter resentment that it was the sheriff and not the woman he wanted.

"What did you want to see me about?" Ash asked, crossing his arms over his chest.

"Uh..." He struggled to organize his jumbled thoughts into a semblance of sanity. "The fire. It was arson."

Ash's lips thinned, nearly disappearing under his beard, which was usually neat but now looked like it needed a weed-whacker to trim. "How do you know that?"

"Because I saw—" He stopped and glanced at the corner again. It was still empty, but now he was doubting himself. Could he trust anything he saw right now? Maybe he hadn't actually seen the figure in the flames, watching everything burn. Maybe it was like Darcy. Not real.

"What did you see?" Ash prompted.

He started to shake his head, but the knife of pain through his skull put a quick end to that. He sucked in a sharp breath.

"I don't know. It might have been nothing, but I thought I saw someone in the barn with me."

"If anyone was in that barn, they're dead now."

"No, he had on turnout gear." Even as the words left his mouth, he knew how crazy they sounded.

Ash made an exasperated sound. "That was Tiago Jimenez. He happened to be driving by when your dumb ass ran back into a burning building, and Sasha flagged him down. He pulled you out of there."

Had he?

Donovan tried to replay those long minutes trapped inside the barn, but it was all jagged images and blurs of movement. "No. No, that's not right. I... I got myself out. I carried Spirit out."

"*Tiago* carried Spirit out, then went back in after you when the roof collapsed."

"No. That's not what happened." He tried to get up, but again, the one-two punch of pain and nausea had him sinking back into the bed. "Ash, I'm telling you. That's not right."

Ash narrowed his eyes. "You have a TBI and a concussion. Your memory is not reliable right now."

Donovan gritted his teeth. He *could* trust his own memories. He had to trust them because without them, who was he? "I know what I saw, and it wasn't Tiago coming to the rescue. Whoever it was, they were just standing there. They were watching the place burn. Enjoying it. I couldn't see his face, but I know the bastard was smiling."

Ash held up his hands in surrender. "Okay, fine. I'll investigate and see if there is any evidence backing up your claim of arson." Sorrow flickered in his eyes, there and gone in an instant. "But, Van, there's already a shit-ton of trouble bearing down on you. Don't make things worse for yourself by telling people that you see things that aren't there."

He wanted to argue, but the fight was draining out of him.

The pain roaring in his head was getting to be too much. He closed his eyes and tried to breathe through it. When he opened his eyes again, he was relieved to see that the corner of his room was still empty.

But then he noticed something else. Sasha still hadn't returned.

"Where's Sasha?" he asked, panic tightening his chest.

"I sent her home," Ash said.

"Why?"

Ash's gaze was molten. "Why do you think? You're poison, Donovan. You always have been. Don't infect her, too."

Donovan gritted his teeth. He was sick of people treating him like he was some kind of disease to be avoided. "You're only saying that because you want her."

"I'm saying it because she's a friend, and I don't want to see her dragged down into your dangerous bullshit."

"*My* dangerous bullshit? I didn't start the fire. I just ran into it to save my dog. And your sister's pet projects."

"You didn't have to do that. You could've waited for help."

"You did it, too."

"Only because Sasha said you'd gone inside. I did it for you, jackass. And instead of staying safe, you ran right back into the flames."

"Yeah, I did. There wasn't time to wait, and losing those dogs would've crushed Anna. I wasn't going to let that happen. That's what friends do, Ash."

"You're not my friend anymore, man. You're just someone I used to know."

Donovan shook his head in disbelief, and the motion nearly made him throw up. He swallowed hard, ordering his stomach to stay put. "You know, for a cop, you're a judgmental asshole."

"And you're just an asshole."

"Fuck you."

"Excuse me?"

"You heard me."

Ash took a step forward, his fists clenched. "You've got a lot of nerve talking to me like that, considering everything you've done."

"And what exactly have I done?" Donovan shot back. He was so fucking tired of being blamed for everything that went wrong in this town.

"You know damn well," Ash snarled.

"Go on. Say it. You think I killed her. You think I killed Darcy."

"I don't think. I *know* somebody killed her because we just found her body burned to a fucking crisp, and I know you were the last person to see her alive."

"Wait." The air left Donovan's lungs like he'd been punched. "You found her?"

"We won't know for sure until the DNA comes back, but yes. We think so."

He leaned back against his pillow and exhaled hard. It might have been a sob, but he wasn't going to own up to it in front of Ash.

They'd found Darcy.

After all these years...

Fuck. This was going to get bad. "I never should've come back to this goddamn town."

"No," Ash said flatly. "You shouldn't have, but you did, and now I suggest you don't try to leave."

If he were smart, he *would* leave before the inevitable arrest happened. But if he left, he'd never see Sasha again.

"I'm not going anywhere." Why should he? This was his home, and he'd done nothing wrong.

"Good," Ash said and turned to the door. "Because we'll be talking again real soon."

part two
burn

When passion is mutual, there is always the danger of the fire burning to ashes.

Beryl Bainbridge

episode 4: the crime scene

Hey there, welcome back to Cold Truth, the true-crime podcast where we dive deep into cold cases to uncover the truth. I'm your host, Alexis Summers, and in today's episode, we're going to talk about a potential crime scene. Specifically, a spot in the woods near Hidden Beach where her shoe was found, and blood was splattered on a tree trunk.

As we previously discussed, Donovan Scott was the main suspect in Darcy Cantrell's disappearance. And while there isn't concrete evidence linking him to the crime, the potential crime scene could provide us with more information about what happened to Darcy on that fateful day.

First of all, let's talk about the location. Hidden Beach is a remote spot in the woods, not accessible by car. To get there, you have to hike around two miles on a path through the woods, and the final descent to the beach is steep and slippery. Not only is it a popular party spot for teenagers, but hikers and nature enthusiasts also frequent it. But they're not the only ones. Because of its remoteness, it's also known to attract some unsavory characters. There have been reports of drug activity and vandalism in the area, so it's not exactly the safest place for an 18-year-old girl to be alone.

And remember: Darcy did leave the party by herself. Donovan followed later, and the estimates of the time gap between the two of them leaving varies greatly—some witnesses say it was a handful of minutes, while others say it was longer, like at least a half hour.

Now, let's focus on the details of the potential crime scene. On the morning of Nov 5th, 2007, a local jogger stumbled upon a red canvas shoe in the woods near Hidden Beach. The jogger reported the discovery to the police, who later confirmed it belonged to Darcy Cantrell.

When investigators arrived on the scene, they immediately noticed something odd about the area where Darcy's shoe was found. The ground was disturbed, large gashes left in the dirt with a scatter of broken twigs and foliage all around. It looked like there had been a struggle, and it didn't end well.

Sheriff Jerry Tennison immediately called in a search team, including cadaver dogs, and they discovered something even more alarming: blood on a nearby tree trunk. The tree was right off the trail the kids used to get to the beach. Darcy absolutely would've passed it if she was going back up to the parking lot to leave. And it wasn't just a little bit of blood, either. It was a significant amount, splattered in a way that suggested it had been flung from something—like a bat? — hitting someone hard in the head. The spatter was tested, and it was later confirmed to be Darcy's blood.

This new information gave investigators a better picture of what may have happened to Darcy Cantrell on the day she disappeared. She was walking away from the beach, ascending the trail toward the parking lot, when she was caught off-guard and hit on the head from behind by a heavy, blunt object. Even so, she didn't go easily and lost her shoe in the ensuing struggle. But we didn't expect anything less from our girl Darcy, did we? She was a fighter right until the end.

Unfortunately, while the discoveries suggested that foul

play was involved, the search was eventually called off due to a lack of more evidence.

And that's it for today's episode of Cold Truth. We've uncovered some startling new evidence that points to a potential crime scene near Hidden Beach where Darcy's shoe was found, and blood was splattered on a nearby tree trunk. It's clear that this case is far from being solved, and we'll keep digging to uncover the truth behind her disappearance.

Thanks for tuning in, and don't forget to subscribe for more updates on this and other true crime stories. Remember to stay curious and stay safe, and keep seeking the truth!

chapter
eleven

IT HAD BEEN two weeks since Darcy's body was found.

Fourteen entire days.

And so far, there had been no mention in the news. Surprising since that fucking podcast seemed to gain new listeners by the day. Ash must have a gag order on his deputies. And it probably helped that the Double R Fire still dominated headlines. It had burned over a hundred thousand acres, destroyed over four hundred structures, and was still chewing up land to the southeast. Every time Cal Fire seemed to have it leashed, it broke the line and kept right on raging, leaving the entire town holding its breath. One shift in the wind and the fire could change course and rip through Steam Valley.

Donovan could see the nerves as he climbed out of his Jeep at the Mad Dog Pub. Townspeople were less polite, and tempers were short. Smoke clogged the air in a yellow haze, turning the sun an eerie red and covering everything in a fine layer of grit. The dry air reeked of burning wood, but it wasn't the pleasant scent of a campfire. It was sharp and bitter and left a metallic taste on the tongue. Everyone wore masks or bandanas to try and keep the shit out of their lungs.

Mad Dog's owner, Rose Galasso, stood behind the bar, hand-drying a rack of beer steins. She looked over at him when the door opened. "Hey, Van. They're all in back. Your usual?"

"Thanks."

"Club soda and lemon coming up." She set down the stein and towel and picked up a tall, narrow cocktail glass.

He studied her as she prepared the drink. She was a beautiful woman, with black hair cut in shaggy layers and shockingly blue eyes. Her breasts strained the fabric of her cropped Mad Dog Pub shirt, and she had almost as many tattoos as he did. She was tough—some might even call her a bitch, but he'd always liked that about her. She seemed like the perfect woman for him, but after one ill-advised night together when he first returned to town, they both realized they'd be better off as friends.

And she'd never revved his engine like a certain shy veterinarian who was avoiding him and dodging his calls. He'd let it slide while he healed, but no more. He was seeing Sasha later today for Spirit's follow-up vet appointment, and he was going to make sure she remembered just how explosive the chemistry was between them.

Rose slid him his drink, drawing his attention back to her. "How are you feeling?"

He took a sip of his club soda and lemon, savoring the tartness on his tongue as he considered how he wanted to answer the question. The news of Darcy's death had hit him hard, harder than he'd care to admit. Part of him had always hoped she did run away like investigators first suspected, escaping town like she'd always dreamed of.

"I'm hanging in there," he said finally. "Mostly healed."

Rose studied him over the bar, her gaze sharp and assessing. Shit, she knew.

"You heard about Darcy?"

She nodded. "The rumor mill's working overtime. People are saying bones were found in the woods off Quarry Road, at the edge of Rawlings' land."

So, soon, everyone would know. Including the press. The fire wasn't going to distract them for much longer. "Thanks for the heads up."

"No problem. You've already been through a lot. If you ever need to talk..."

He appreciated the sentiment but shook his head. "Thanks, Rose, but I'm not much of a talker." It was true he preferred to keep his emotions to himself. It was something he'd learned early on, growing up in a household where vulnerability was seen as weakness.

She smirked. "Which is why you go to therapy, right?" She tilted her head to the back room. "I think they've already started."

He raised his glass to her. "Yeah, figure that one out. A bunch of wounded vets with substance abuse issues meeting in a bar to talk about our feelings and shit."

She laughed. "These are strange times we live in."

"The strangest. Thanks, Rose." He made his way toward the back room, the sound of hushed voices growing louder as he approached. The therapy group used to meet at Redwood Coast Rescue, but obviously, that wasn't going to work for a while. The Mad Dog was the only other place in town with an available room that wasn't a church—they preferred to keep the meetings secular.

This would be his first time back since the fire. He'd been coming to these meetings for a few years now, so why was he nervous? He took a deep breath and pushed open the door, stepping into a circle of men and women all seated on mismatched chairs and bar stools.

Dr. Amelia Firestone ran the therapy sessions. She was a

smartly dressed woman with silver-streaked hair and had recently started wearing stylish, black-rimmed glasses. She was soft and kind like a grandmother and yet somehow managed to handle a room full of stubborn, hotheaded veterans with the skill of a matador.

She smiled warmly when she spotted him. "Donovan! Welcome back."

All eyes turned on him.

Zak, seated next to Dr. Firestone, lifted his chin in greeting.

Next to him sat Sawyer Murphy, a fellow Marine who was semi-blinded when a sniper's bullet got past his helmet and fucked up his brain. He could still see movement, but as soon as that movement stopped, he was sightless again. On the floor between them was Zelda, Seeing Eye Dog extraordinaire. She'd traded in her tutu from the fundraiser for her typical service dog vest with a handle on the back.

"Oh, great," Sawyer said. His voice was laced with sarcasm, but he was grinning. "Grumpy's back?"

"Hey, someone has to counteract your sunshine and rainbows optimism, Daredevil."

Sawyer snorted a laugh. "Pretty sad that I'm considered the optimist in this group."

Beside Sawyer was Pierce St. James.

"You okay?" he signed, his forehead creased with concern. He'd lost his ability to speak due to shrapnel severing his vocal cords, and the whole group had learned ASL so he could participate in their sessions without feeling isolated.

In their world, isolation was a killer.

"I'm good," Donovan assured and grabbed a bar stool from the stack in the corner.

Pierce's eyes narrowed.

"For real, man. Stop looking at me like I'm gonna break. It'll take more than a fire and a bump on the head to get rid of me." To prove it, he grinned at the group and held out his arms. "Miss me?"

"Like a case of the clap," Zak deadpanned.

"Ew," Veronica Martens said. She was seated at Dr. Firestone's other side and didn't usually talk much during their sessions. She looked at the doctor with disgust. "Why are men so gross?"

"Okay, enough joking around," Dr. Firestone said, taking charge of the conversation. "Let's start with check-ins. Who wants to go first?"

They went around the circle, each person sharing their struggles and successes from the previous week and Donovan let himself relax into the familiar routine. He'd missed this, missed these people who understood what he'd been through and didn't judge him for it.

But as the session wore on, his thoughts kept drifting to Sasha. He wanted to see her, touch her, feel her. He needed to know if they still had a chance. Maybe he'd ask her out for dinner during Spirit's appointment, or maybe he'd just kiss her and see what happened.

He was a man of action, after all.

"Donovan?"

He blinked. Shit. How long had his mind been wandering? By Dr. Firestone's tone, it wasn't the first time she'd said his name.

"Sorry." He shook his head and remembered too late, it wasn't a good idea. He'd told Rose the truth—he was mostly healed, the burns on his arms and chest now fresh pink scars, marring his tattoos. But his head was still all kinds of fucked up.

Or more fucked up than usual.

At least he hadn't seen Darcy's ghost again since the hospital.

Annd he still hadn't spoken, which had everyone in the room looking at him with varying degrees of concern.

He opened his mouth, but found he didn't know what to say. Did he mention the hallucinations? No, better to keep that to himself.

Finally, Dr. Firestone spoke again, her eyes kind. "I'm sorry to hear about the possible discovery of Darcy's remains."

His heart nose-dived into his stomach, but he tried to shrug it off like it was no big deal. "I'm glad she was finally found."

"Are you worried about the sheriff's investigation?"

"I'd rather not talk about it."

"Okay, that's okay." Dr. Firestone shifted gears smoothly. "Why don't you tell us about your injury?"

"The fire? There's nothing to tell."

"No. Your TBI. I don't think you've ever told us how it happened."

His chest constricted as he glanced around at the group. "I'm sure I have."

"Nah," Zak said. "At least, not since I joined."

Pierce shook his head.

"Yeah, I haven't heard it," Sawyer agreed.

"Your turn," Veronica said with a mean sort of glee in her dark eyes. "You forced me to tell my story. You're not getting away without telling yours."

He rubbed his palms on his jeans. Panic, his old friend, wrapped its arms around his chest and squeezed. He wasn't ready to talk about it. He'd never been ready to talk about it with anyone. But he'd been coming to these meetings for years, and he owed them something. They'd all shared their stories, they'd all bared their souls to one another. It was only fair that he did the same.

Donovan took a deep breath, closing his eyes for a

moment before he began. "We were supposed to sweep and clear an insurgent hideout. Routine shit, or so we thought." Suddenly restless, he popped to his feet and ran a hand over his buzzed hair. "But then I found that fucking door. It was booby-trapped, like always. No big deal. I had disarmed hundreds of those things before. But this one was different. This one had something else, something I didn't see until it was too late. A secondary device."

The memory plowed into him like a train, sending him right back to those mountains. He swore he felt the ground shake under his feet again. He could taste the dust in his mouth, could hear the screams of his men. The coppery scent of blood and the acrid scent of fuel mixed in an overpowering stench that he could still smell. It was forever branded into his nose.

Dr. Firestone's voice was soft, coaxing. "What happened, Donovan?"

"It exploded." The words came out strangled and he cleared his throat as he sank back to his seat. "I don't remember much after that. Just bits and pieces. There was a lot of smoke, and it was hot. I remember feeling like I was on fire. And having just been on fire, I can confirm it still sucks."

Zak winced. "Not funny, Van."

"Too soon," Sawyer agreed.

"Go on," Dr. Firestone prompted. "What happened next?"

Tears prickled at the back of his eyes, but he refused to let them fall. He was a Marine, dammit. Marines didn't cry. "I don't know. I was... I was thrown. Like I said, I don't remember much. Just pain then...nothing. We never knew what kind of explosive they used in that second device, but it was powerful. It killed two guys on my team and left me with my brain scrambled."

He didn't want to talk about it anymore, but the group was silent, waiting for him to continue.

Several seconds ticked by and he couldn't stand silence. His ears always started ringing again when a room was too quiet, so he filled it with more words: "Ammonium nitrate is a common explosive used by insurgents. It's odorless, which is why it's so hard to detect. They mix it with other explosive materials to make it even more deadly. I smelled kerosene right before, so maybe that's what it was. Ammonium Nitrate Fuel Oil. Just good old ANFO. The tried and true method to get rid of pesky American infidels. Or it could've been—"

"Donovan," Dr. Firestone interrupted gently. "Do you blame yourself for missing the second device?"

Donovan's head snapped up, and he stared at her for a long moment before he answered, his voice hoarse. "Every goddamn day."

"You know it's not your fault, right?" Pierce signed.

He scowled at the guy. "I should have seen it, but I didn't. And because I didn't, I failed my team, killed two men, and fucked up my head so badly I'm seeing my dead ex-girlfriend in the corner of this fucking room." He stared at her. Darcy smirked and wiggled her fingers at him.

Everyone else turned to look at the corner, then looked at each other in shock.

But not Dr. Firestone. She nodded as if she had expected that answer. "It's okay to feel guilty, Donovan. It's a normal reaction to a traumatic event. And hallucinations are a common symptom of TBI, especially when you're under stress. And you're under a tremendous amount of stress right now, on top of suffering another concussion. But it's important to remember that what happened in Afghanistan wasn't your fault."

He snorted. "But what happened to Darcy was?"

"I didn't say that," she said, her voice even.

"You didn't have to. I see it all over your face." He stared at the group, and betrayal cut through his gut like a blade. He stood up abruptly and his stool crashed to the floor. "Fuck this. I'm done here."

As he strode from the room, he could feel the weight of their stares on his back.

He didn't need this therapy shit. He didn't need to be reminded of all the things he had lost. He just needed to forget. He slowed as he passed by the bar, where Rose was laughing with a patron. He could walk over, set down his empty glass, and ask for a real drink. Then he'd forget...

"Hey, Van," Zak called. "Wait."

No.

Fuck.

What was he thinking? He'd been sober for almost three years and wasn't going to blow that streak now. Not over this.

He turned away from the bar and faced the man who was once like a brother to him. "If you're going to say—"

"Yeah, you don't want to hear it, so I should save myself the breath. But I'm saying it anyway. We're here for you, man. We've all been through some shit, and we're all still standing." He smirked and tapped his metal leg. "Even if it's with some extra help. You don't have to face any of this alone. You have a solid support system in the team. Use it."

Jesus, he was suffocating. He needed air. He needed to get out of there.

Without another word, he shoved through the pub's door. The smoke had gotten worse while he was inside. It stung his eyes and scraped the back of his throat with every inhale. He looked at the unnatural yellow glow over the mountains. It was afternoon. The sun was to his back, making its slow descent toward the ocean. That glow was all fire, and it looked closer than before.

The whole fucking world was burning, and he wanted a

drink. He wanted to sink into the seductive arms of alcohol and drown his sorrows and forget.

But he refused to throw away three years of sobriety.

The vet clinic where Sasha now worked was just down the road. He smiled to himself and strode for his Jeep.

There were other ways to forget.

chapter
twelve

"HEY, MARY-LISA?" Tablet in hand, Sasha stepped out of the treatment room and approached the reception desk where her Jill-of-all-trades receptionist had set up shop. "I need you to contact Coco's mom with an estimate. I just went over the bloodwork with her and let her know I'm seeing a few things that have me concerned. Coco's liver enzymes are elevated, and her white blood cell count is also high, which makes me think there's some kind of infection in there, but I'm not sure if the infection is causing the liver issues or vice versa. I'd like to schedule an abdominal ultrasound to get a better look at her liver, and I'm also going to start her on antibiotics to treat the infection. I'll want to run another CBC after the course of antibiotics, but—"

The door to the clinic opened, and she lost her train of thought as Donovan stepped in with the energetic Spirit at his side. It was the first time she'd seen him since Ash told her to leave the hospital, and he looked good. Of course, she knew he was healing. Anna had kept her apprised of his recovery, but seeing him now, healthy and whole, lifted a weight off her shoulders she hadn't even realized she'd been carrying.

"But...?" Mary-Lisa prompted, glancing up from her computer.

"Oh. Um." She moistened her suddenly dry lips and stared down at the tablet. Coco's chart might as well have been in a foreign language for all the sense it made. She blinked and forced herself to focus. "Right. Sorry. Forgot what I was saying."

Out of the corner of her eye, she saw Donovan smirk.

She ignored him. "Um, so Coco's mom is concerned about the cost. Can you work up an estimate for the ultrasound and antibiotics and give her a call? You might want to add in the second CBC, too, so she's not surprised by it."

God, why was the room suddenly too small, the air too hot? She glanced at Donovan again but turned away when she felt heat creeping into her cheeks. Donovan's gaze lingered on her for a moment longer, his eyes searching her face. She couldn't read his expression, and it made her uneasy. She turned back to Mary-Lisa, trying to ignore the flutter in her stomach.

"Sure, I'll take care of it," Mary-Lisa said. "Is there anything else you need from me before I go to lunch?"

"No, that's all, but it can wait until this afternoon. Go ahead and lock up. I just have one more patient, then I'll take my lunch in my office."

She turned to Donovan with a bright smile. Her customer service smile. It pulled at her cheeks and only softened when she gazed down at his dog. "Hello, again, Spirit."

Spirit side-eyed her hard and pressed closer to Donovan's legs. Funny—the dog loved her when she wasn't wearing the white lab coat, but whenever she had it on, she suddenly became Public Enemy Number One. She straightened and faced Donovan again. "If you'll follow me?"

He nodded and followed wordlessly to an exam room.

When the door shut, he finally spoke. "Hi, angel."

Oh, God. He was right there, directly behind her. She could feel his breath on the back of her neck and his voice was like a caress down her spine. Her nipples peaked uncomfortably against her bra.

She turned to him and found herself pressed against his chest.

"Good to see you up and about," she said, trying to sound casual. "How's your recovery going?"

He skimmed his knuckles over the curve of her cheek. "You can drop the customer service act. I'm not a customer."

She glanced down at his dog. "She's my patient. You're her owner. That makes you a client."

Donovan leaned closer, his lips almost touching her ear. "Why did you disappear on me in the hospital?" His thumb brushed over her bottom lip, and she parted them slightly.

"I didn't want to intrude," she said breathlessly.

"You could never intrude." He leaned in, his lips just a hair's breadth away from hers. "I've been thinking about you, angel. Dreaming about you."

Her heart was pounding so hard she could barely hear him over the rush of blood in her ears. She shivered at the feel of his breath on her skin, her body reacting to him in a way that she couldn't control.

"Donovan, please," she whispered, trying to push away from him.

But he held her in place, his hands reaching around to grip her hips. "Please what?" His voice was low and husky, sending a shiver down her spine. "'Please keep touching me like this?' 'Please show me how much you've missed me?' Because I have missed you, angel."

She closed her eyes, the sensations he was evoking overwhelming her. She could feel his erection hardening between them. He wanted her just as much as she wanted him.

"I—I have to examine Spirit."

"No, you don't. She's fine. All healed. I'd be the first to tell you if there was a problem."

As if to prove his point, Spirit huffed before strutting over to the door and pawing at it. When it didn't open, she sat down and glared at them like, *"Can we go already?"*

"She does look good," Sasha conceded. "Her burns have healed nicely, and I can see she's already growing hair back. But, Donovan, I can't—"

"You can and you will." His mouth swooped down and claimed hers in a kiss that was tender and fierce all at the same time. His tongue slid into her mouth, caressing and tasting her.

God, she'd missed him.

Her arms went around his neck, her fingers scrubbing over his short hair as she deepened the kiss, her body pressed tight to his. He pulled her hips closer, and she rocked against him, feeling him hard against her belly.

Donovan broke the kiss and pressed his lips against the sensitive skin below her ear. "I need you, angel, so much. I need to feel you, to know you're with me again."

She heard the front door shut as Mary-Lisa left for lunch and closed her eyes. Was she really going to do this here, at work? And not even at her own clinic, but her mentor's—the place she'd started her veterinary career at?

Yes.

She took Donovan's hand. "My office."

His grin was all smug masculine pleasure. "Lead the way."

Spirit sulked after them as she pulled him through the treatment room to the small office in back.

As soon as they were inside, Donovan pushed her against the door, his mouth hot and demanding on hers. She moaned, her fingers digging into his shoulders as he lifted her up and she wrapped her legs around his waist. His mouth left hers and trailed hot, sucking kisses down her neck and collarbone, his hands caressing her ass through her scrubs.

She arched her back, rubbing herself against him. "Donovan..."

"I know, angel," he murmured against her ear. "I've got you."

She gasped as he dropped her back to her feet and spun her toward her desk.

"Hang on to something."

"Why?" She tried to look at him, but he kept her turned away with one hand on her back, pressing her against the desktop. His fingers dipped under the band of her scrub pants and her legs wobbled. She grabbed the edge of her desk as he pushed a finger into her.

She heard the door open at the front of the clinic, and voices carried back. She froze. "Oh! Wait. We can't. Someone's back from lunch already."

"Then..." He brushed her hair aside and kissed the back of her neck, sending a cascade of chills over her skin even as fire ignited in her belly. "You'd better be silent."

A second finger joined the first, pumping until she was soaked, and a needy moan slipped from her mouth. His free hand slid up around her neck and clamped over her mouth as his fingers left her channel to circle her clit.

She felt trapped, caught between the desk and his hard body as he tortured her in all the most delicious ways, and she didn't want to escape. She clawed the desktop and cried out against his palm.

Donovan laughed softly, his breath a warm caress on the side of her neck. "You're not staying silent. You want me to make you come right here at work, don't you, my naughty angel?"

He lightened the pressure on her clit. Balancing on the tip

of climax, she whimpered and grabbed for his hand, desperate to keep his fingers there.

"But if I finish you off now, will you still be ready for me later?"

Oh, God. She'd never not be ready for this man. All he had to do was look at her from across a room and she needed a change of panties. But she couldn't tell him that because of his hand clamped over her mouth, so she ground her butt against his erection. He growled, buried his face against her neck, and gave her what she needed. He held her tight as she exploded.

"Fuck," he breathed and removed his hand from her mouth. "I want to lay you down on this desk and fucking ruin you."

You already have.

That thought brought her back to herself, and she stepped away from him, adjusting and retying her pants. She trembled all over with the aftershocks of orgasm, but tried to keep the quiver out of her voice. "That was... very unprofessional."

He smirked. "Spirit didn't mind."

She glanced over at Spirit, who was watching them from the dog bed in the corner. The border collie actually rolled her eyes, and the huff she gave was full of disgust. "I think she minded quite a lot."

"Ah, she just doesn't like sharing me." He snaked an arm around her and pulled her against his hard body. He was still turned on, the ridge of his erection straining the front of his jeans. "Come over later."

Not a question but a self-congratulatory statement.

She sighed. "Donovan—"

He silenced her with a hard kiss. "Don't say no."

God, she was so screwed. There was no way she could say no to him. She'd never been able to say no to him.

If she indulged tonight, would he still be in her bed come morning? It felt like there was a big black hole in her chest.

"I'll try."

He frowned. "Try?"

"I can't promise—"

"I'm not asking you to promise anything. Just show up."

She nodded.

"Good." He kissed her again and called for Spirit, who popped to her feet with an eager swish of her tail. He started for the door, but paused with his hand on the knob and frowned at her desk. "Is that all you're eating for lunch?"

"What?" She looked at the protein shake and apple, and her cheeks flushed. "Um, yeah. I'm on a diet."

"Hm." His frown deepened into a scowl as he left.

Sasha drew a shaky breath and sank into her desk chair, every nerve ending still tingling with the aftereffects of being so thoroughly satisfied. Desire made her want to press her hand to the juncture of her thighs and rub to relieve the ache already growing there again. But she couldn't do that. She had to eat lunch and catch up on charting. She had hospitalized patients to check on and six more appointments this afternoon. She had to pull herself together.

Okay.

She straightened her clothing, blew out a breath, and smoothed back her hair. She could do this. And she'd worry about Donovan Scott later.

chapter
thirteen

THE DRIVE HOME was filled with Sasha and Donovan loved it. He could still taste her kiss and her scent was all over his clothes. He'd loved burying his face in her hair as he kissed her neck and stroked her to climax.

He grinned.

He had so many plans for her tonight, but that was hours away still, and he was too keyed up to sit around waiting until she got off work. He cleaned the house, but it didn't take long. He was too much of a Marine still to be a slob. He changed the sheets on his bed and threw in a load of laundry, then checked the time.

It had only been a half hour.

Jesus.

He rolled his shoulders, but it didn't help to relax him. It had been a long time since he felt this psychically charged, like a taut rubber band about to snap. He needed to work off some excess energy or else he'd break his bed when he finally got Sasha into it.

He looked at Spirit. She sat by the door with her leash in her mouth. Her tail thumped hopefully.

"Fine. We'll go for a quick run." With the haze of smoke in

the air, it'd suck more than usual, but he couldn't deny the dog's utter joy at the word "run" and chuckled as she went crazy with excitement. She streaked back and forth across the living room, using the couch as a trampoline to launch into her bed by the fireplace. She grabbed the dog bed and tossed it into the air, then in a blur of black and white fur was on the couch again. The cushions squeaked as she hopped back and forth like her paws were spring-loaded. She'd been cooped up in the house too long while she healed. She deserved the run. They both did. He'd stick close to the coastline, where the smoke wasn't too bad.

Donovan clapped his hands. "C'mon, let's go run."

Spirit barked and hopped over the back of the couch, skidding to a stop in front of him.

"Ready, girl?"

She impatiently tapped her feet as he grabbed his phone and keys. He looped her leash over his shoulders like a bandolier. He didn't expect to need it, but the fire had him nervous. He didn't know how she'd react if one sparked nearby and wanted the ability to keep her close.

He opened the door, and they took off, jogging together down the hill toward the beach where his life started falling apart.

By the time they reached the sand, Spirit had worn herself out from doing laps around him the entire way. She collapsed and rolled in the surf, letting the waves lap at her sides.

Donovan sat on a piece of driftwood and looked out to sea as he willed his breathing to even out and the stitch in his side to ease. That had been a rough run, his first since he'd been cleared by his doctor two days ago. He was going to need a minute to recover. Luckily, Spirit didn't mind. She loved the beach.

As he watched the waves break against the sea stacks, he thought about Darcy, and the last time he'd seen her here on this beach. His heart ached for the girl he'd let walk away so long ago. He'd never stopped thinking about her or wondering what had happened to her.

And now he finally knew.

Darcy was dead.

Murdered.

Grief gathered in the back of his throat like a sob. He swallowed it down. He was an adult; he was a warrior. But part of him still loved the damaged girl Darcy had been. That was the worst thing of all. He was pathetic.

He shoved his hands in his pockets and dug his knuckles into his thigh to distract himself from the pain in his gut. Maybe if he ignored it, it would go away. Or maybe he could finally fix this, the worst of his mistakes. Maybe he could make it right. Maybe...

There was no maybe.

Spirit, soaked and sand crusted, nudged his leg with her nose and whined at him.

"I'm okay, girl." He took off his running shoes and walked down to the wet sand above the tide line. With the wind blowing inland, there was almost no smoke. He could breathe here and savored the clean scent of the ocean.

Cold water lapped at his ankles, but it did nothing to cool the turmoil inside him. He'd never allowed himself to grieve for Darcy. It had felt wrong when he hadn't known her fate. For fifteen years, fifteen long years, he'd held out hope that maybe, just maybe she was still out there somewhere. And now that he knew she wasn't, the pain was almost unbearable.

But here, in the place he'd last seen her alive, he could mourn. He could say goodbye. He needed to say goodbye if he wanted more than a series of hot hook-ups with Sasha. He needed to be a better man for her. He needed to be worthy of her.

He stood there longer than he expected, lost in his grief until his feet went numb in the cold water. Then he drew a breath and swiped at his eyes with the backs of his hands. Spirit sat at his side, staring up at him with concern. He reached down to rub her head.

"I'm okay now. Really."

She eyed him with obvious doubt. If dogs could talk, she'd be saying, *"Yeah, right, dude. You're a mess."*

"Ah, but I'm your mess, sweetheart. Aren't you a lucky dog?" He glanced out over the ocean again, but this time, he didn't feel the crushing weight of grief or regret any longer. He turned back to his dog. "Let's go home and get you dinner. Sasha's coming over tonight, so you'd better behave, you hear me? Show her what a good girl you are."

Spirit huffed and flounced on ahead of him, her tail swishing haughtily. That was probably a no, but he decided to take it as a yes. She'd come to love Sasha. How could she not? The woman was sweet, funny, and sexy as hell with all those curves she hated. She was also strong, with a backbone of steel hidden behind a facade of shyness. And she had a heart the size of California that she gave out to friends and animals indiscriminately. He hoped there was a little piece available for him. He knew Spirit already had one.

Halfway up the path, his skin suddenly prickled with goosebumps, and he stopped moving.

Something was wrong here.

He stared into the woods, searching for the source of the off-note. But nothing moved, and Spirit didn't seem alarmed as she nosed through the brush on the side of the path. And, still, he couldn't shake the feeling someone was out there, watching him.

He cursed under his breath and pinched the bridge of his nose as a headache roared to life in his skull.

Just paranoia, he told himself. It was just another fun side effect of his TBI, like the headaches and hallucinations and memory lapses.

Spirit popped up out of the brush, carrying something in her mouth. She trotted over to him, tail wagging, so proud of herself for her find.

"Hey, girl. What do you got there?" He knelt and held out a hand. "Let me see it."

And she dropped a woman's red canvas shoe into his palm.

chapter
fourteen

SASHA HADN'T EXPECTED to find Donovan on her porch when she got home. She'd done her best not to think about him all afternoon and now, here he was, sitting on her steps, his motorcycle parked in her driveway.

"Hi," she said cautiously and stepped out of her car. "I thought I was coming to your house."

"I wasn't sure you knew where I live."

"It's a small town. I could've figured it out."

"Okay. I wasn't sure you'd come." His voice had a strange hollow note in it that was concerning.

She walked over and picked up his helmet, placing it on her lap as she sat beside him. "You made it very hard to say no."

"Yeah," he whispered. "I can be a pushy bastard when I want something."

"I'm not complaining." She studied his profile as he stared out at the gathering dusk on her street. She could tell he wasn't seeing the three other houses she shared this cul-de-sac with. "What's wrong?"

He laughed but there was no humor in it. "Do you want a list?"

"No, I don't need one. Darcy," she guessed.

He said nothing for five solid seconds, then exhaled hard and hung his head, scrubbing his hands over his short hair. "Ash told you to stay away from me because of her. You should listen. He thinks I'll poison you, too."

She hesitated only a beat before lacing her fingers through his. "No, you're not poisonous. You're not colorful enough."

He looked at her, surprise obvious in his dark eyes.

"Aposematism," she explained. "It's the conspicuous markings or bright colors animals develop to warn predators of toxicity. The brighter the colors, the more toxic. Now if he'd said you're venomous..." She tilted her head, considered. "That I might believe."

A smile twitched at the corner of his mouth. "Want me to bite you and find out?"

She patted his hand. "Pretty sure you already did that, and I survived, so not venomous either."

The tension eased out of his shoulders as he leaned in and kissed the side of her neck, sending a cascade of shivers through her. "We might want to try it again. You know, for science."

Oh, God, she wanted to pull him inside and take him to bed, but her protein shake and apple hadn't been enough for lunch, and she was starving.

She let him nibble at her neck for a moment longer, then shifted away. "Dinner first."

Even as she said the words, her stomach gave an embarrassingly loud growl.

He swore and stood, lifting her to her feet. "I'm taking you out."

"I'd like that."

"Good." He started to pull her toward his motorcycle, but she resisted.

"Oh, wait. You mean, like, right now? I have to change out of my scrubs. And feed my dog."

He paused. "You have a dog?"

"Matilda. I asked Anna if I could adopt her after the fire."

Without releasing her hand, he changed directions and went to her door. "How is she?"

"Scared. You know, with all the smoke in the air, it's probably like a never-ending flashback for her." It was a little difficult to dig her keys out of her purse one-handed, but she managed it. Donovan took the keys and unlocked the door, holding it open for her to go in first. "I've been keeping her in my laundry room with an air purifier running, just hoping to mitigate some of the trauma."

His expression darkened. "If I ever meet the bastard who tied that sweet baby to a tree and set her on fire, he'd better run. Fast. Because if I catch him, I'll tie *him* to a tree and see how he likes it."

"He deserves it and worse. I just don't understand how anyone could harm a defenseless animal like that."

"It takes a special kind of evil." He stayed by the door as she crossed through her kitchen to the laundry room.

Matilda wagged a tentative greeting, but when she spotted Donovan, she went still like a deer in headlights.

They didn't know for sure a man had tortured her but assumed as much by the way she cowered whenever a man was near—unless it was Zak. He'd worked with her as she healed, and she adored him. But all other men terrified her, which, dammit, Sasha should've considered before she opened the door and let her out.

Except then Matilda did something amazing. Her tail started whipping the air, and she made happy little crying sounds as she crawled toward Donovan.

"Hi, pretty girl." He knelt and opened his arms to her.

The dog threw herself at him, wiggling and whimpering with joy.

"Okay," Sasha said, stunned. "Wow. She really loves you. She must understand that you saved her."

"Yeah, well, we're survivors aren't we, Mattie? Like recognizes like." He showered the dog's muzzle with kisses, and Sasha's heart melted into a puddle. If she weren't already falling hard for this man, she would have plummeted right then.

After one last kiss on her scarred nose, he straightened. "Tell you what. You go shower and change, and I'll run home for Spirit. I'm sure Matilda would enjoy the company."

Twenty minutes later, she was waiting out on her porch in jeans, boots with short heels, and a black wrap blouse that camouflaged her belly while still giving flirty glimpses of her cleavage. She'd spent way more time standing in front of her closet deciding on an outfit than she normally would, but now she worried she'd gone too casual. Or not casual enough? Or too flirty?

She heard the growl of his motorcycle before he turned onto her street. She'd expected him to switch to his Jeep since he was bringing Spirit back with him—but nope. Spirit rode behind him with her paws up on his shoulders, wearing a dog-sized helmet and goggles over her eyes. Her ears flapped in the wind while her tongue hung from her mouth in a wide doggie grin of excitement.

"You taught your dog how to ride a motorcycle?"

His eyes sparkled as he took off his helmet. "Well, she is my dog, and this is my primary mode of transportation in the summer. Of course she rides with me." He climbed off the bike and unstrapped Spirit from her harness. She jumped down and zoomed in happy circles around the yard.

Sasha watched with a grin. "You two are good for each other."

"Yeah, we are. I've even forgiven Zak for manipulating me into taking her."

"That's how you ended up with her?" She laughed and shook her head. "Why am I not surprised?"

He whistled for his dog. Spirit streaked over to him in a black-and-white blur, but sat patiently as he removed her helmet and goggles. He ruffled her ears. "All right, girl. Let's go in and say hi to Matilda. Your mission tonight is to keep her company and make sure she doesn't get scared."

Spirit's whole demeanor changed. She went from bouncy puppy to work mode. If dogs could salute, Sasha had no doubt Spirit would.

Donovan tossed her a treat from his pocket. "Good girl."

"Wow. Does she speak English?"

"When I tell her she has a mission, she knows she needs to listen up." He led Spirit inside. When he returned a few minutes later, his eyes roamed appreciatively over her. "You're testing my control with that outfit, angel. Ready to go?"

Heat rose to her cheeks. "Yes."

She had no idea where they were going, but she couldn't care less. As long as she was with him, nothing else mattered. He laced his fingers through hers and pulled her down to the driveway.

When she realized where he was headed, she put on the brakes. "Why don't we just take my car? It's going to be dark soon and—"

"You can ride a motorcycle in the dark. That's why it has this." He tapped the headlight and grinned. "C'mon, I know you have a naughty risk-taker in you. I saw her at the fundraiser."

Now the heat in her cheeks was an inferno. "That wasn't me. Not really."

"I think it is." He held out his helmet and nodded toward

the orange glow above the mountains. "C'mon. Don't you want to live a little before this fire burns us alive?"

She scowled and snatched the helmet from his hand. "That's really not funny."

"Wasn't trying to be." He took the helmet back and fitted it over her head. "I learned a long time ago that life is too damn short not to live it to the max. If you spend every day worrying about the what ifs, you miss all the spontaneous beauty of the right nows." He lifted the visor and leaned in to kiss her nose. "And some things are worth the risk."

She eyed the Harley suspiciously. "I don't know that a motorcycle is one of those things."

"That's because you've never ridden one. Don't trust me?"

She shouldn't. All the evidence said she shouldn't. But, dammit, she did. She trusted him with her life—which, if she got on that motorcycle, would be in his hands.

Donovan swung a leg over the seat, his muscles flexing as he kicked back the kickstand and straightened the bike. He'd changed clothes, too, and now wore a leather jacket over a plain T-shirt and jeans. She admired the way the leather wrapped his biceps. He looked like a man who worked hard for what he had, and that made her feel even more self-conscious. She tugged at the neck of her shirt, trying to hide her ample cleavage. She worked out—not consistently, but she wasn't a complete couch potato. She also tried to eat well, but she had a sweet tooth and loved ice cream. She'd always been chubby as a kid, and it just seemed like no matter what she did, she was destined to remain a chubby adult.

So why did he want her when he could walk into a gym and have his pick of women? She decided right then she'd renew her gym membership.

He patted the seat behind him expectantly.

"Oh, God." She drew a breath and climbed on, wrapping her arms around his waist and pressing her body tightly against his. His low growl of approval was drowned out by the throaty grumble of the engine.

"Hang on tight, angel," he said over his shoulder, and before she had a chance to second-guess this idea, he gunned the throttle.

The bike shot out of her driveway, and Sasha let out a squeak of alarm. She pressed her helmet against his back, squeezing her eyes shut. Because of the helmet, she couldn't hear his laughter, but she could feel it shaking his chest.

She couldn't help but laugh despite her nerves. This was insane. She was on the back of a motorcycle, holding onto a man who made her heart race. It was exciting and terrifying all at once.

As they tore down the winding road along the ocean, Sasha's grip on Donovan tightened. The wind tugged at her clothes and the roar of the engine was deafening, but her fear slowly turned to exhilaration. The thrill of the ride was overwhelming, and she was intoxicated by the adrenaline coursing through her veins. She opened her eyes and looked around, taking in the scenery. The sun was setting in the smoke-hazed sky, casting an eerie red-orange glow over the ocean.

Donovan was right - this was the right now, and it was beautiful.

He steered the bike into a sharp curve, leaning deep into it, and Sasha pressed herself tighter to him, savoring the hardness of his back against her breasts and the sensual vibration of the engine between her legs. A shiver raced through her. She had never felt so alive and yet so vulnerable before, but she wanted to feel more. She slid her hands down his stomach, fingers dipping into the waistband of his jeans.

She smiled against his spine at the growl that rumbled through him and trailed her fingers lower. He shifted slightly, allowing her more access. Her heart pounded as the tips of her fingers brushed against the hardening length of him. She knew she shouldn't be doing this while on a motorcycle, but the thrill of the moment was too much to resist. She squeezed him gently and he let out a low moan.

Donovan turned his head slightly, his eyes meeting hers over his shoulder. The corners of his mouth lifted in a smile, but there was a hint of warning in his gaze. She was treading on dangerous ground, but she couldn't help herself. She wanted him in the worst way, hadn't stopped thinking about him since his visit to her office this afternoon.

The bike slowed as they pulled up to a scenic turnoff hidden from the road by a line of trees. Donovan shut off the engine and turned to face her, his eyes smoldering with desire. He pulled off her helmet and tossed it aside, then cupped her face in his hands and leaned in. His lips captured hers in a heated kiss as his hands roamed over her body, igniting a fire within her as dangerous as the one on the horizon. If she wasn't careful, it would consume her, but he tasted of adventure and risk, and at that moment, she didn't care if she went up in smoke.

Sasha broke the kiss, gasping for breath. Donovan's hands were still busy, exploring every inch of her body, and she could feel herself growing wet with desire. She wanted him so badly it hurt.

"Donovan," she whispered, her voice shockingly husky with need. She'd always had a low, throaty voice, but now it sounded downright sexual.

He lifted his head. "What do you want, angel?"

"I want to suck you."

She'd startled him. Actually, she'd startled herself, too. She'd never been so honest about her desires with past lovers.

He gripped her shoulders and eased her back. His eyes were dark and intense as he stared at her, his breathing as ragged as hers. Then he groaned. "Jesus. You're trying to kill me."

She stroked her fingers down his shaft again and reached to unbutton and unzip his jeans. He moved his knees wider apart, giving her room. With one hand, she squeezed his erection and with the other, she cupped his balls, weighing them in her hand. She leaned down and licked the drop of pre-cum off the head of his cock. He shuddered, and she did it again, this time flicking her tongue over the head.

His fingers delved into her hair. "Fuck. I can't take much more of that."

She gave him a wicked smile. "You can take more."

And she sucked him into her mouth.

She had never been so bold before, but this was Donovan and he brought out a boldness in her that she'd never known existed. She became a shameless slut, giving him oral sex on the side of the road. She'd had no idea she had it in her, but she loved it.

This was nothing like when she'd made love with previous boyfriends. This was fiery and intense, and she wanted to consume him. She wanted to suck him dry.

She could feel him watching her, his gaze eating her up with so much desire that it made her wetter. She stroked his shaft faster, working him with both hands, and taking him as deep as she could. He tasted so good, a salty sweetness, and she craved more.

As she took him deeper and deeper into her mouth, he started to moan.

Donovan tried to pull her off, but she only gripped his hips tighter and held on. She loved the feel of him, the taste of him, and loved how powerful she felt. She dragged her tongue along the underside of him, licking from root to tip until he was shaking in her arms. She lifted her gaze and found him watching her with eyes that had gone black with hunger. He groaned and his muscles tensed. She was going to make him—

His hands tightened in her hair, pulling her head back

until her lips were no longer touching him. "I want to come in your pussy, angel." His voice was all growl. "Not your mouth."

In one swift movement, he lifted her off the bike and turned her to face it. Sasha watched over her shoulder, her heart racing with anticipation, as he stripped off her jeans and took himself in hand, probing at her entrance. She licked her lips and pressed her hips back against him, moaning as he entered her in one slow stroke. She was slick and hot for him and took all of him.

Her hands curled around the edge of the leather seat as he withdrew almost completely and then pushed into her again.

He groaned. "Do you have any idea how often I've thought of doing this to you again?" She could hear the raw desire in his voice as he punctuated each word with a thrust. "Every day, every fucking hour, since the night of the fundraiser. Even when I was in the hospital, I lay in that bed at night and fantasized about you."

"Oh, God, Donovan. Me too. I couldn't stop."

"Did you touch yourself when you thought of me?"

"Yes." She spread her legs as wide as she could, and pushed her ass back against him, meeting him thrust for thrust and loving the way his breath grew ragged.

"Touch yourself now."

She didn't move.

He nipped at the back of her neck. "I'm not going to let you come if you don't touch yourself."

She squirmed against him as a wave of frustration washed over her. She was so close, but he kept pulling back when she needed harder and faster. "Ugh! You're a horrible lover."

He chuckled. "Yes. But I'm *your* horrible lover. Now, touch yourself."

She glared at him over her shoulder. "No."

He stopped moving, his cock deep inside her. "No?"

"You touch me."

"Deal. But you'll pay for it." He reached around her front and found her clit, rolling it between his fingers. She whimpered as the familiar tingle began deep inside her.

"That's it, angel. Come for me."

Her orgasm hit her hard, spiraling out of control within seconds, and while she was still riding the high, he withdrew from her and spun her around, dropping to his knees in front of her. She swayed on her feet. Donovan gripped her thighs and pulled her down until her butt touched the bike seat, then he buried his face between her legs.

She cried out as he sucked and stroked her swollen clit in the same rhythm he'd been using to fuck her. He was as relentless as he was merciless, bringing her back to the edge of orgasm twice and then stopping, leaving her a gasping, trembling puddle.

"Donovan." His name left her lips in little more than a whimper.

He nibbled her inner thigh. "Now, what do you want, angel?"

She ran a trembling hand over his head. "You. Inside me. Right now."

Donovan grinned and kissed his way up her body. When he reached her lips, he softened the kiss to a tease. "Will you touch yourself when I ask next time?"

"Yes," she breathed.

"Good girl." He turned her back toward the bike, kicked her legs wide, and filled her again. He grabbed her hips, fingers biting into her skin, and shifted his angle, his thrusts became more urgent, wilder. She leaned forward, resting her forearms against the seat, and met him thrust for thrust. When the orgasm hit her, it was all she could do to stay upright, her body shaking hard with her release.

He dropped his head to her shoulder and groaned, his

fingers digging into her hips as he pushed into her one final time, deep and hard, and shuddered.

He wrapped his arms around her and pressed his face to her spine. She could feel his heart beating wildly against her back as their ragged breathing slowly evened out. Her body felt boneless, and she was only vaguely aware of their surroundings. She was leaning over a bike seat on the side of a highway, with his cock still deep inside her, but it didn't matter.

"Jesus, Sasha," he whispered, his voice raw. "I'm never going to get enough of you."

He kissed her shoulder and her neck, but there was no urgency to it. He was kissing her, touching her like she was a precious gift, not a trophy. She'd never felt so cherished in her life.

They stayed like that for several long, comfortable minutes until her damn stomach let out another embarrassingly loud grumble.

"Oh, fuck. You need food." He withdrew from her and straightened, reaching down to help her from the bike. "I got distracted."

"Me, too." She sighed and melted into his arms and raised her mouth to his in a kiss that tasted of sex. "Worth it."

Just then, Donovan's stomach joined hers in voicing its disapproval. They stared at each other for a beat, then burst out laughing. He tucked himself back into his jeans and waited for her to pull herself back together, then held out her helmet. "C'mon. Let's go eat."

chapter
fifteen

THEY MADE it to the restaurant on the outskirts of town much later than anticipated, but that meant they had missed the worst of the dinner rush. Donovan felt a bit shaky as they were seated, but whether that was from his lack of food today or the mind-blowing sex, he couldn't begin to guess.

Sasha's cheeks were flushed, and her hair was mussed. She looked exactly like what she was: a well-loved woman. As he watched her study the menu, he decided he wanted to make her look like this every day for the rest of his life.

Yeah, he was a goner.

He loved her.

Hell, if he were honest with himself, he'd loved her from the second he'd first set eyes on her at Redwood Coast Rescue. His memory sucked most days, but that moment he remembered with the clarity of a photograph. He had been needling Zak after a group therapy session, trying to get a rise out of the guy because Zak's sudden Zen attitude had bugged the hell out of him. The side door leading out to the agility yard swung open, and Sasha and Anna came in with Matilda on a leash. They were deep in a discussion about the dog's recovery, but Sasha had glanced his way as they passed. It had been like a punch to the gut, all of the air forcefully leaving his lungs, and he devoured every detail from her dark hair in its bouncy ponytail to the curvy hips and ass that tested the limit of her scrub bottoms. Her smile was so bright and genuine, he was dazzled and swore his heart had skipped a handful of beats. He hadn't even known her name yet, but he'd known she would be his.

She was smiling at him the same way now and lowered her menu. "What?"

He shook his head. "Just thinking about the first time I knew you were mine. You had on the same pink scrubs you were wearing today."

"When was that?"

"You and Anna had taken Matilda out to the agility yard to exercise, and you were talking about how well her burns were healing with a lot of medical jargon—which is hot as fuck. I was with Zak in the kitchenette behind the reception desk, and you smiled at me."

Her eyes rounded. "But that was over a year ago."

"I was waiting for the right time to make my move."

He didn't think it was possible, but her eyes got even wider. "The fundraiser. Oh my God, that wasn't a fluke, was it? You had a hotel room. You kenneled Spirit for the night and got a room at the casino. That whole time, you were planning to seduce *me*?"

"Well, the plan came about after Zak blackmailed me into going, but... yeah. I went there with the intention of getting you into my bed. I was tired of waiting for you to notice me."

Sasha's mouth dropped open, and he worried for a moment that he'd said something wrong. But then she started laughing, a deep, throaty sound that had him grinning in response.

"And I went there thinking I'd seduce Ash! We both had seduction plans."

A few weeks ago, the man's name would've sent a spear of jealousy through him, but this relationship they were building felt too damn secure for Ash to rattle. "Glad I won."

Her eyes softened as she reached across the table for his hand. "Me, too."

He held on to her for a moment, then regretfully pulled his hand back and picked up his menu again. "What do you want?"

"A burger. A big, juicy burger with cheese and bacon and all the bad-for-you stuff. But..." She sighed. "I'll probably get a salad. My diet, you know?"

Yeah, he wasn't about to let her do that. When the waiter came to take their orders, Sasha did indeed order a salad. He ordered two bacon cheeseburgers with fries.

"Wow," she said as the waiter walked away. "Hungry?"

"Yeah, but one's for you."

She groaned. "Donovan, I'm trying to be good."

"I don't want you to be good. I want you to be fed. You're gorgeous the way you are, and I hate the thought of you starving yourself to fit someone else's definition of a beautiful woman." He leaned across the table and lowered his voice as the hostess led a group of men past their table. "Besides, we burned a helluva lot of calories earlier, and I have plans to burn more when we get home."

Her cheeks flushed a charming pink, and she opened her mouth, but he never got a chance to hear her reply.

"Donovan? Donovan Scott, is that you?"

One of the men broke away from the group and walked over to their table. He was tall and leanly built, with deep-set dark eyes and a sprinkling of gray at his temples.

"Tiago." Donovan stood and met Tiago Jimenez's

outstretched hand with his own. "Hey. I hear I owe you one for making sure I didn't end up barbecued."

The Hispanic man threw his head back and laughed. It was a big sound, too loud for the hush of the restaurant, and drew several glares from other patrons. "Yeah, you're just damn lucky my date went so well that night, or else I would've already been home asleep." He turned his charming grin on Sasha. "Speaking of dates, I don't believe we've met."

Donovan glanced back and forth between them and wondered if his scrambled brain was playing tricks on him again because they must have met. Hadn't Sasha flagged him down during the fire? Then again, that night had been crazy. It was possible Tiago just didn't recognize her now.

Sasha narrowed her eyes in question at him, and he realized a beat too late that his silence had gotten awkward.

She stood and offered her hand. "Hi. I'm Sasha LeBlanc."

"Oh, right. The vet. My sister—" Tiago broke off, and a deep, heavy grief flashed in his eyes before he hid it. He determinedly plastered his smile back in place, but it was less charming now, strained around the edges.

Donovan's heart clenched with a brief, hot spike of sorrow. Before succumbing to her heroin addiction, Chrissy Jimenez, Tiago's sister, had been part of the Paws for Vets therapy group, trying to work through the sexual assault she'd suffered at the hands of a superior officer while in the military. Her death had been a blow to them all because she had seemed to be one of their success stories, then, out of the blue, she stopped coming to the group. Less than two weeks later, she was dead from fentanyl-laced heroin.

Tiago cleared his throat. "Sorry. My sister's cat was a patient of yours."

Sasha nodded, radiating empathy. "Yes, Gizmo. His new owner still brings him to see me. I was very sorry to hear about Chrissy's passing. I liked her."

"Everyone loved her." He stared at Donovan for an uncomfortably long moment. "Isn't that right?"

His throat constricted. "Yeah."

Chrissy had been one of those people who drew others to her with her bubbly personality and radiant smile. Even after the trauma she experienced while in the Army, followed by an addiction to painkillers that eventually led to heroin, she never lost that sparkle.

Donovan had been drawn to her, and they'd become fast friends. They would've been more if circumstances were different when they met, but at the time, they had both been supremely fucked-up individuals barely holding themselves together. Neither could've spared the emotional bandwidth for a relationship, though they had both wanted one. They'd flirted, dancing dangerous circles around each other right up until a couple of months before Chrissy's death.

He swallowed back the lump of guilt suddenly blocking his throat. He hadn't thought about Chrissy once since Sasha came into his life. "I never got the chance to tell you how sorry I am about Chrissy. I saw her just a few hours before and she seemed like her usual self. I wish she would've told she me she was struggling. I wish I'd have seen it."

A dark shadow passed over Tiago's face. "She knew the risks every time she stuck that needle in her arm, but she didn't stop."

"I wanted to help her."

"Yeah, man. We all did." He sighed and glanced over to the table his friends had settled at. "I'd better get back. We're headed out to the fireline tomorrow, so this will probably be our last good meal for a while. Sasha, nice meeting you." He nodded to her, then clapped a hand on Donovan's shoulder. "And you stay out of burning buildings, *comprende*?"

"Yeah, you don't have to worry about that. It was a one-time deal. I'm not pressing my luck again."

When Tiago was gone, Sasha sank back to her seat and studied him over the table with concern in her eyes. "That upset you."

He nodded. No sense in hiding it. "Chrissy was a good friend."

"Tiago seems to think you two were more than friends."

"He might think so, but it wasn't like that. Chrissy and I liked each other. We flirted—a lot. But I was still fighting a losing battle with my demons, and she had hers. We both knew if we took that step beyond friendship, it'd destroy us."

"That was very rational of you."

He tapped his temple with one finger. "Yeah, well, when your brain's full of holes, sometimes all you can do is cling to the remaining rational bits and hope they're enough to keep you afloat."

Her expression softened, and he glanced away, staring hard out the window. Unfortunately, it was dark enough outside that all he could see was his own reflection, but that was better than the pity he knew was in her eyes.

The waiter arrived with their dinners, and they both picked at their plates in uncomfortable silence.

"You know, I'm not the only one with issues," he said finally.

Sasha raised an eyebrow. "I never said you were."

"Zak had more issues than Playboy."

She exhaled a soft chuckle and popped a fry in her mouth. "True."

"And I saw Ash a little bit ago. He looks like hell."

"He has a lot on his plate."

"Yeah, and I just loaded on more," he muttered and scowled down at his dinner. He'd lost his appetite. "Can't decide if I shot myself in the foot or not."

"What happened?" When he hesitated, she reached over

the table and squeezed his hand. "You don't have to tell me anything you don't want to."

He lifted his head and met her gaze. Instead of pity, he saw understanding, which was somehow worse. "I want to tell you everything. I just don't know that I should. I don't want you to think less of me."

"Hey." She squeezed his hand again. "If this is about Darcy, I know you didn't kill her."

"Then you'd be one of the few people in town to think so." But, he decided, he would tell her the truth. She deserved to know everything about the man she was sleeping with—even the bad parts. "Before we came over this afternoon, Spirit and I went for a run to the beach to burn off some of her energy. We hung out down there for a bit—maybe forty-five minutes. We didn't see anyone else around, but on the way back up the trail, she found a red shoe."

Sasha inhaled. "Like Darcy was wearing when she disappeared?"

"Exactly like that. It couldn't have been hers, though. It was too new, too clean. But I contacted Ash, and he took it into evidence. I'm sure it was someone's sick idea of a joke. They saw me out running and decided to put the shoe on the path to torment me."

Her brows drew together. "But it's not like people just carry red canvas shoes around with them. That seems very deliberate. What does Ash think?"

"I already told you what he thinks. Even if he's not convinced I'm a killer, he still doesn't think too highly of me."

"Why? You used to be so close. I remember the three of you—You, Zak, and Ash—were inseparable in high school."

He lifted a shoulder and raised his glass to his lips. "We grew up, grew apart."

"No, it's more than that. What happened?"

"It's..." He set his glass down without drinking. "There

was a night a few months before everything happened with Darcy. We were out doing stupid teenage shit, and the sheriff caught us. He threw us in county lockup and threatened all kinds of charges, from trespassing to criminal mischief. Zak's parents came for him, and the sheriff let him go with barely a warning. Ash's parents came, and same thing..."

When he trailed off, she nodded in understanding. "But not you."

"My parents didn't come. Even if they had, I doubt the sheriff would've let me go. I'm not town royalty like Ash or from a respected family like Zak. I was just trailer park trash. The kid from a broken home on the wrong side of the tracks, who would probably not amount to much. The sheriff even said so. He said he expected to see me behind bars more often than not."

"He was wrong."

"But that's the thing—he wasn't. At least, not then. I was on a bad path. All three of us were, but Ash and Zak had get-out-of-jail-free cards because of their last names. They had more chances to get right than I did. That night, sitting by myself in a jail cell, I realized if I stayed in town after graduation, the sheriff's words would come true. A self-fulfilling prophecy. I'd end up hitting the revolving doors of county lock-up just because of who I was and where I came from and because nobody expected anything more from me. So, I stopped talking to Ash and Zak and enlisted in the Marines."

"And then Darcy," Sasha said. It was a matter-of-fact statement, not a question.

"Yeah, and then Darcy disappeared, and I thought, fuck, I'm too late." He gave a rough laugh and shook his head. "The sheriff eyed me right from the beginning and I was sure he was going to railroad me into a life sentence. But he never made the arrest. I graduated, went off to join the Marines, and never planned to look back."

"So why did you come back?"

Grief clamped a hand around his windpipe and made speech impossible for a long moment. "My mom. She had breast cancer and needed help. I was a mess myself, but—I came home for her. I started going to therapy for her. Got right for her and took care of her until the end."

"Did she pass recently?"

He sucked in a sharp breath and wondered if it would always hurt to think about his mom. "March. She, uh, actually went into remission for a bit after I came home and was doing great—and then she fell and broke her wrist, and they found that sneaky shit had come back and spread to her bones. She was gone less than three weeks later. She was only fifty. She should've had so much life left."

"I'm so sorry." She picked up a napkin and tore off a small piece of it, then another and another until she had a little pile in front of her. "I lost my dad when I was seventeen, days before my eighteenth birthday."

"Does it still hurt? Because I can't think of Mom without my chest seizing up." He thumped a fist to his chest. "Even the good memories hurt."

Sasha reached for another napkin and started shredding it, too. "I know what you mean. My dad used to take me fishing with him every summer, and I loved it. But now, every time I see a fishing pole or a crab pot, all I feel is sad. It does get better, and the good memories become a little more sweet than bitter, but it never goes away. I still miss Dad every day."

Donovan caught her hands mid-rip and set the napkin aside, then turned his palm toward hers and laced their fingers together. "Tell me about him. What was he like?"

"Oh." She laughed softly. "He was larger than life, you know? He had an infectious laugh and really kind eyes, all wrinkled at the corners. His hair was all white—I never remember it any other color—and he wore it long, in a ponytail down his back, but when he woke up in the morning, it stood up every which way, like he'd been shocked in his sleep."

"He sounds like a good man."

"He was, but he had his demons, too. Like so many of the fishermen around here, he drank too much and partied too hard when he was on shore. But he never neglected me. I always came first when he was home, and he showered me with affection—I think because he felt guilty for being away for weeks at a time and leaving me with a nanny."

It was similar to his and Darcy's childhoods, he realized with a start. But also so very different because Sasha probably always looked forward to her dad's return from the sea, while he and Darcy had always dreaded theirs. "Where was your mom?"

Sasha shrugged. "Who knows? She left when I was five or six. Dad was quite a bit older than her, and he made a good living—had his own fleet of boats—so she probably had visions of being a trophy wife when they got married and didn't realize what she'd actually signed up for. He served in Vietnam and struggled with depression, PTSD, and suicidal thoughts. Eventually, Mom couldn't take it anymore and moved to LA, chasing dreams of stardom, I guess. She just left and forgot she had a husband and daughter. Not that I think life would've been better with her there. She was young and didn't want the responsibility. So, it was just Dad and me against the world."

Just like him and his mom after his dad died. He cherished the memory of those fear-free days, as short as they were. "That sounds nice."

"It was for a while. He always told me I was his rock. I was what kept him going..." She trailed off and stared out the window at the parking lot. He felt her drifting too far away from him, back into dark memories, and squeezed her hand.

She looked at him and gave a sad smile. "But, in the end,

even I wasn't enough. He shot himself, and I've always felt guilty because I wasn't there. I was supposed to have been there. He was on shore, and we'd made plans for the weekend, but I canceled at the last minute to go to San Francisco with a friend."

Now he was starting to understand her obsessive need to plan everything. She thought she could mitigate heartache with a checklist.

"Angel," he whispered and waited until she looked at him again. "If he was in that dark of a place, it would've happened whether you were there or not. You hit that edge, and it's almost impossible to pull back from it."

Her eyes swam with tears. "Have you ever been at that edge?"

He should lie. He knew he should, but found he couldn't. Not to her. "Yeah. I was right there, staring over."

"But you pulled back."

Shit, he shouldn't have said anything. He sighed heavily and stared hard at the table between them, unable to meet her eyes. "No, I didn't. The gun misfired. I reloaded to try again, but the phone rang—Mom calling to tell me she was sick. Her cancer is the only reason I'm alive right now."

"Donovan," she said softly and tightened her grip on his hand. "Promise me, if you ever get to that edge again, you'll talk to me. Or if not me, then Zak. Or Sawyer. Pierce. Veronica. Dr. Firestone. Even Ash—just someone. Promise me."

He stared into her eyes and gratitude overwhelmed him in a rush. This woman, who had suffered so much herself, was offering him a lifeline.

"I promise," he said, his voice hoarse with emotion. "I won't keep it inside again."

She studied him with a mix of concern and tenderness, then finally nodded. "Good. I believe you."

Jesus, he loved her. He wanted to pull her across the table

and kiss her, to feel her soft lips against his, to forget everything else in the world. But he knew if he started, he wouldn't be able to stop, so he settled for raising her hand to his lips and kissing her knuckles instead.

"Eat, angel. Your food's getting cold."

episode 5: the interrogation

Hey, Truth Seekers! Welcome back to another episode of Cold Truth. In the last episode, we talked about the potential crime scene where Darcy Cantrell's shoe was found along with blood splattered on a nearby tree trunk. Today, we're going to cover the interrogation of Donovan Scott by Sheriff Jerry Tennison. So grab your coffee, and let's listen to part of the recording.

[Sound of interrogation room door opening and closing]

Sheriff Tennison: Mr. Scott, thanks for coming in today.

Donovan Scott: I didn't have a choice, did I?

Sheriff Tennison: Don't you want Darcy found?

[Silence]

Donovan Scott: [softly] Yeah.

Sheriff Tennison: We just want to ask you a few more questions about the night she went missing. Can you walk us through your movements that night after the party?

[Sound of Donovan shuffling in his chair]

Donovan Scott: I left shortly after Darcy stormed

off. I tried to find her, but she was already gone. I figured she got a ride from someone, so I went home.

Sheriff Tennison: Alone?

Donovan Scott: Yes.

Sheriff Tennison: And you didn't try to contact her after that night?

Donovan Scott: No. I was pissed. I didn't want to talk to her.

[Sound of papers shuffling]

Sheriff Tennison: Mr. Scott, you know why you're here today?

Donovan Scott: No.

Sheriff Tennison: We found blood at the scene where Darcy Cantrell's shoe was discovered, and it matches your blood type. Would you like to explain how that happened?

Donovan Scott: That's not possible. I wasn't there.

Sheriff Tennison: Well, your blood was.

Donovan Scott: Then someone planted it!

Sheriff Tennison: C'mon, Donovan. This isn't a movie. Look at it from my position. You were arguing with her at the party. Witnesses say that you were visibly upset, and that Darcy pushed you away.

Donovan Scott: We had a disagreement. She hit me, but I didn't lay a hand on her.

Sheriff Tennison: That's not what we heard from some witnesses. They said they saw you and Darcy walking toward the woods together. And then, a short while later, they heard a woman screaming.

Donovan Scott: [angry] Fuck them! They were all drunk. I didn't take her into the woods. I told you, I left alone. I never saw her again.

Sheriff Tennison: Okay. Did you stop anywhere

on your way home? See anyone that could give you an alibi?

Donovan Scott: The gas station on Main and Fourth. I bought a bottle of water, a bag of chips, and cigarettes. Check the cameras.

Sheriff Tennison: We do have surveillance footage that shows you at the gas station alone, but you hung out there for a long time. A suspiciously long time—long enough that the night clerk worried you were working up the courage to rob him.

Donovan Scott: No! I just didn't know what I wanted. And I didn't want to go home yet.

Sheriff Tennison: Did you return to the beach later that night?

Donovan Scott: Why would I?

Sheriff Tennison: See, here's what I think happened. You followed Darcy into the woods to try to make amends after the fight, and things got heated again. Maybe you pushed her, and she fell, hit her head, and didn't get back up? I bet that made you scared, with you all set to join the Marines after graduation. The military won't take a murderer. So, you hid her, went to the gas station to establish an alibi, then went back after the party was over and buried her. All you gotta do is tell me where she is, and this will all be over."

Donovan Scott: I didn't hurt Darcy. I love her. I wanted to marry her until that night.

Sheriff Tennison: You don't still want to marry her?

Donovan Scott: She turned me down.

Sheriff Tennison: And that made you mad, didn't it?

Donovan Scott: Why do you think we fought?

Sheriff Tennison: Mad enough to hit her? Did you take your baseball bat with you to the beach that night?

Donovan Scott: What? No! Jesus, I'd never do that to her or any woman. I'm a fuck-up, but my mom taught me better than that.

Now I'm going to stop the recording here because the interrogation goes on like that for several hours, with the sheriff throwing out theories, trying to wear Donovan down. But the kid never wavers in his story. It seems like he might even have a solid alibi, but the evidence found near Hidden Beach still raises too many questions.

One quick note: the blood Sheriff Jerry mentions did not actually match Donovan's blood type—it matched Darcy's—so the sheriff was either mistaken or purposely bluffing about that in hopes of getting a confession.

So, could Donovan be telling the truth? He sounds sincere enough, but we know from past cases that skilled liars often come off as the sincerest witnesses until something finally breaks through their facade.

But we also have to consider the possibility that Donovan is innocent and someone else may have been involved in Darcy's disappearance. There were a lot of other kids on the beach that night. Is there another viable suspect we haven't considered yet?

Join us next time as we keep digging for answers. Until then, I'm Alexis Summers. Stay curious, stay safe, and keep seeking the truth.

chapter
sixteen

ASH RAWLINGS SANK into his office chair and closed his eyes, letting his head fall back, and his shoulders relax.

Half his county was burning, and the other half just hadn't caught fire yet.

He was running on fumes, and he didn't see an end in sight. Cal Fire was losing the battle with the Double R and had called in smoke jumpers and hotshot crews from as far away as Alaska. Towns to the east and south had been evacuated, and he'd had to deal with two dipshit looters in Shasta Springs last night as the fire raged toward town. His overtime budget was maxed out, and his department was spread impossibly thin.

And, on top of it all, he had a flaming hot cold case sitting on his desk that he hadn't even had the chance to look at. He could probably put it off until the worst of the fire threat was over, but he didn't dare. He wanted to have something concrete before the story broke because, thanks to that podcast, it was going to be a media circus.

Groaning, he dragged his hands over his head and sat up, jiggling his mouse to wake the computer. He needed to go home, get some sleep, but even if he tried, he didn't see it happening. He was too wired, so he might as well take the next few hours to go over the initial investigation into Darcy Cantrell's disappearance—especially since he didn't have much to go on for his own investigation yet. The fire had threatened the county morgue, so he'd had the body flown to San Francisco for an autopsy. So far, he hadn't received results. He imagined she was low on their priority list since it was an old case, and they probably wouldn't get much information from a pile of charred bones.

An uneasy chill tapped-danced down his spine at the memory of those bones being loaded into a body bag. The blackened skull with its blank eyes and macabre grin was going to haunt his nightmares for years to come.

That skeleton used to be Darcy.

A girl he'd known since kindergarten.

A girl he'd dated very briefly during one of her and Donovan's many breaks. Those two had been off more than they were on. They were a toxic match, but something kept pulling them back together—until she disappeared.

Jesus. He really didn't want to think Donovan had anything to do with it, but he'd been at that party on Hidden Beach. He'd been a year older than most of the kids there, graduated but still figuring out what he wanted to do with his life. Amanda, his girlfriend at the time, had dragged him to the party. He'd seen the explosive fight between Donovan and Darcy and heard Donovan's drunken rants about how she'd "be sorry." He'd watched Donovan storm off into the woods after her.

But was Donovan capable of hurting her?

No. Not the Donovan he'd once loved like a brother. He knew that without a shadow of a doubt, but he also knew alcohol changed people. Donovan's father had been proof of that. Rooster Scott had been an affable, well-liked man when he was sober but was mean as a snake when drunk.

Donovan had drunk a lot the night of the party. He'd played multiple games of beer pong and flip cup, knocked back several rounds of shots. If he was anything like his father, it was possible he hurt her in a fit of rage while under the influence of all that alcohol.

A pit opened in Ash's stomach as he navigated to the right file in the department's database— *2007 Missing Person/ Suspected Homicide- Cantrell, Darcy Megan.* He opened the report and started reading through the initial investigation.

It was thin.

Hell, downright emaciated.

"What?" He rubbed his eyes and scrolled through it all again. Maybe he'd missed something due to exhaustion or—

Nope. That really was the whole thing. At least, it was all he had. An entire investigation boiled down to a few short reports, a single recorded interview with Donovan—and not even the first one Sheriff Jerry conducted—and a handful of crime scene photos. There was no DNA, no fingerprints. He didn't even know what evidence the former sheriff had used to secure the initial search warrant for Donovan's house.

This couldn't be all.

Ash had worked with Sheriff Jerry for years before the guy retired. He had a reputation for toughness, holding his deputies to the highest of standards, and he was a thorough investigator. Ash had seen him as a mentor, and this kind of sloppy police work wasn't like him at all.

Ash reached for the phone on his desk but stopped when he remembered it was almost midnight. And that was when he hit a wall, physically and mentally. He groaned and rubbed at the back of his neck with both hands. He had to shut down for a few hours, or he was going to crash.

Tomorrow. He'd call Jerry first thing and get this sorted. And he had to bring Donovan in for another interview.

He again reached for the phone. Got it all the way to his

ear before he remembered the time and dropped it back into its cradle.

Tomorrow, he reminded himself.

Darcy had already been dead for fifteen years. As much as it bothered him to wait, one more night wasn't going to make that much of a difference to her.

chapter
seventeen

"WELL, LOOK WHO'S BACK," Zak said, completely unsurprised, as Donovan stepped into the room minutes before the therapy session was scheduled to start. "What happened to, and I quote, 'fuck this. I'm done here?'"

"Told you, we always come back," Sawyer said. "I'd say it's like an abusive relationship, but it's kinda the opposite of that."

"Feels abusive sometimes," Pierce signed.

Donovan ignored them all and took his seat without a word.

"Welcome back, Donovan," Dr. Firestone said gently. "How have you been?"

Her expression was pleasantly blank—did they teach that expression in shrink school? —but he could still see the doubt in her eyes. And maybe a little fear. She thought she was talking to a man who had gotten away with murder.

Shit. He shouldn't have come back, but he was here because—well, this ragtag group of veterans was all he had for friends. And with Sasha at work and the rescue out of commission, he was bored.

He forced his jaw to unlock. "I've been good."

"Just good?" Zak prompted with a knowing smirk.

Donovan flipped him off, but there was no heat in it. "Yeah, okay. Better than good. I'm in my first real relationship since before my TBI, and it's..." He couldn't think of the right word. "Beautiful" came to mind, but the guys would laugh at him if he said that, so he settled on: "Amazing. She's amazing."

He couldn't help but smile as he thought of Sasha. They'd spent every night of the last week together, sometimes at his place but usually at hers. He loved going to bed with his arms around her every night and waking her every morning with soft, slow lovemaking. He enjoyed flexing his rusty culinary skills to make her lunch every day because he hated the thought of her trying to survive on a protein shake and a piece of fruit. Her eyes always lit up when he walked into the clinic, like she was surprised he'd come. He hoped that in forty years, she'd still look at him like that when he brought her lunch.

"He has little hearts dancing around his head, doesn't he?" Sawyer said. "I can hear them doing the samba."

"He's a goner," Pierce said. *"First Zak and now him? Is there some kind of love flu going around?"*

Because Sawyer could still see movement, he usually understood most of Pierce's sign language, but not today. "He's a what?"

"Goner," Donovan supplied, amused despite himself. "He said I'm a goner. And fuck you, dude. I'm gonna put money down on you catching that love flu next."

Pierce's eyes bugged. He shook his head and waved his hands in the universal signal for *oh, hell, no!* Then he signed, *"I'm perfectly happy with my bachelorhood, thank you. And Raszta doesn't like strangers."*

"How is the mop dog doing?" Zak asked, settling back in his seat.

Pierce had taken in Raszta, a Hungarian Puli, to train for

urban search and rescue when they started their little doggie A-Team a few months ago. The dog's coat formed natural dreadlocks, and he looked like the love child of a bear and a mop.

"Razzy's the best." Pierce's face grew animated as he signed, which was weird because the guy almost never cracked a smile. *"He's crushing his disaster certification training. My disability has slowed us down, but we're figuring ways around that."*

"That's fabulous," Dr. Firestone said. "I'm so happy both you and Raszta have found a purpose."

"He's exactly what I needed to keep going," Pierce said.

"Spirit, too," Donovan said. "I wouldn't be in a position for a relationship with Sasha now if it wasn't for her."

"Is this the part where I say I told you so?" Zak asked, then his grin dropped away. "Man, I miss having the dogs here with us."

"I miss Alfie," Veronica murmured, speaking up for the first time all session.

Donovan had to admit he missed the little guy, too. Dr. Firestone's psychic Papillon, with his butterfly ears and psychedelic bowties, had always been a great comfort during these sessions. Alfie always knew who most needed some snuggle therapy, which made the heavier stuff easier to discuss. He definitely could've used some Alfie comfort during the last session. Maybe then he wouldn't have let his temper get the best of him.

"I'm working on finding us a more permanent meeting spot that allows all the dogs and not just Zelda," Dr. Firestone said. "But until then, we have to respect the health code here—"

"Uh... hey, guys?" Rose cracked the door open and poked her head in. "Sorry to interrupt, but you might want to see this."

Donovan's stomach dropped like he was on the first hill of

a rollercoaster, but there was no corresponding rush of adrenaline to make the feeling better. It was all dread.

They got up and followed Rose out to the bar, where she picked up a remote and increased the volume on one of the TVs.

"Breaking news this afternoon, as authorities have discovered a body in the woods near the town of Steam Valley. The body is believed to be that of missing eighteen-year-old Darcy Cantrell, who disappeared in 2007. However, an autopsy and DNA testing will be required to confirm the identity of the remains. According to sources, firefighters found the body in the ashes left by the devastating Double R Fire, which could make identification more difficult."

They showed the picture of Darcy that had been used time and again since her disappearance—a school photo of a smirking girl with dyed-black hair and flat eyes lined in heavy black makeup. It looked like a mugshot, and it wasn't the real Darcy. It didn't show her wicked sense of humor or the big heart and bravery that compelled her to stand- up for the outcasts.

"Darcy Cantrell's disappearance has been the subject of a popular ongoing podcast," the anchor continued, "and a vocal group of fans recently started an online petition demanding answers as to why investigators' main suspect, Donovan Scott, remains at large. While it is too soon to say what led to Miss Cantrell's disappearance and possible death, this discovery is a tragic development for a community already devastated by the wildfire—"

"Turn it off," Donovan said and sank into a chair at one of the high-top tables. He scrubbed his hands over his head. "Fuck."

"What can we do?" Sawyer asked.

Donovan lifted his head to stare at the three men. Veronica, as usual, had hung back and still hovered by the door to the back room. "Does anyone have a time machine?"

"If I did, I wouldn't be stuck using sign language to communicate," Pierce signed.

"And I wouldn't be blind," Sawyer said.

Zak stared pointedly down at his metal leg.

"Yeah, okay, I get it." Donovan chuckled, but there was no humor in it. "Fresh out of time machines."

"What if we investigate ourselves?" Zak suggested. "Our tactical K9 program is on hold until the rescue is rebuilt, so we have nothing but time on our hands and we have the skills. Pierce and I could poke around town while Sawyer does some research online—"

"I do love internet sleuthing," Sawyer said.

Zak gestured toward him in a sweeping motion, a nonverbal, *"See?"*

Donovan held up his hands. "Slow down, Uno. How is poking around town and reading a bunch of true crime blogs gonna help? And Ash won't like it."

"Fuck Ash. What?" Zak asked when everyone just stared at him. "He's my brother-in-law. I'm allowed to call him out when he's being a jackass. We were all friends once—hell, basically brothers—but I haven't seen him doing jack-shit to help clear your name."

"Because," Ash said with barely restrained patience as he pushed through the front door of the pub, "my job isn't to clear his name. It's to find the truth."

Rose scoffed and gave up on wiping down the bar. "Yeah, okay."

"Do you have a problem with me?" Ash snapped, which surprised the hell out of Donovan. He glanced at Zak, who whistled softly and backed up a step, hands raised as if to say, *"Nope, I'm staying out of this."*

Ash was usually a stoic man, quiet and shuttered, communicating mainly in grunts—unless it was with his sister. Anna was the only one who could get under that hard outer shell he'd built around himself. Except, apparently, Rose Galasso could, too, because Ash was simmering with aggravation now as he planted his feet, crossed his arms, and faced off with her. He looked rougher than he had when Donovan saw him earlier in the week, with his hair sticking up from multiple agitated passes of a hand and heavy shadows darkening his eyes. The fire and investigation were getting to him, fraying his nerves.

Someone needed to slow him down before he self-destructed.

"Yeah, you know, I do have a problem with you, Sheriff." Rose slung the towel over her shoulder and planted her hands on her hips. "You talk all high and mighty about truth, but the sheriff's department doesn't exactly have a stellar reputation when it comes to finding the truth, especially when dealing with society's most marginalized people."

"Maybe that was true under the last administration," Ash admitted, though it seemed to pain him to do so. "But I'm going to start changing things around here."

She rolled her eyes. "Good luck with that. Do you even *know* this town? Have you ever actually sat down with any of the people here and asked them how they want things to change?"

"No," he said, voice tight, his patience obviously on its last fraying thread. "I haven't exactly had time for fireside chats."

"Make the time."

"Oh, sure. I'll add it to my to-do list right after I corral the media, figure out who killed Darcy Cantrell, and protect everyone from this wildfire—which, it was just confirmed five minutes ago, was started by arson, so my list just grew exponentially longer because now I have to find a fucking arsonist. But be honest, Rose. You can't really be too concerned with the state of our town and its marginalized people when you opened a pub here to profit off our rampant alcoholism."

"Oh, fuck you." She snapped the towel off her shoulder and stormed away, slamming her office door hard enough to rattle the bottles on the shelf behind the bar.

"Yikes," Pierce signed.

"That sounded like a conversation Zelda and I want to nope out of," Sawyer agreed and started toward the door with Zelda leading the way. "See you guys next week. Unless you do decide to investigate, then I'm in."

Ash swung toward the remaining group, his eyes intense as a muscle twitched under his beard. "Nobody here is investigating any-fucking-thing, got it?"

Zak gave a noncommittal shrug and also walked toward the door. Pierce hesitated, then followed.

"I mean it, Hendricks!" Ash's voice boomed after them. "We may be family now, but that won't stop me from throwing your ass in jail for obstruction."

"Your sister will love you for that," Zak called back, unperturbed.

Ash groaned and pinched the bridge of his nose like he had a raging headache. "Of all the men she could've married..."

Dr. Firestone took the long way around Donovan but patted Ash's arm soothingly as she passed him. "You know he just likes pushing your buttons, Sheriff. Don't let him see how much it bugs you, and he'll eventually stop."

"Easier said than done, Doctor."

"I know." She gave a sympathetic smile as she left.

The front door clicked shut, leaving Donovan and Ash alone in the bar.

Donovan was still waiting for that next rollercoaster hill. It was going to be a killer when it finally came, and he suspected Ash was here to push him over the edge. "So... the fire was arson?"

Ash paced a few steps, his hands bladed on his hips. "Yeah. Someone doused the back of the barn in accelerant and struck a match."

"At the risk of sounding like Zak—I told you so." But he couldn't find any joy in being right. "There was someone in the barn with me that night."

Ash parted his lips to protest, but Donovan held up a hand, stopping him.

"And it wasn't Tiago coming to my rescue. I don't know why he lied, but I saved myself, and Sasha didn't know him. We saw him out to dinner the other night, and she didn't recognize him as one of the firefighters she flagged down. You need to talk to him again because his story isn't adding up."

Ash growled and continued pacing. "Don't tell me how to do my job." After several minutes dragged by in silence, he stopped moving, took a deep breath, then finally met Donovan's gaze. "I need you to come in for questioning regarding Darcy."

There it was—the second rollercoaster drop. And this hill catapulted him straight into his worst nightmare. "Are you arresting me?"

"If I were going to arrest you, you'd be in cuffs already. This is just a routine follow-up."

"Routine, my ass." He thought of the chicken teriyaki rice bowl he'd asked Rose to store in the fridge under the bar. He was already running late to take it to Sasha for lunch. "Does it have to be right now?"

"No, but I'd appreciate it if you could make an appointment with my secretary within the next two days." Ash dug a card out of his wallet and held it out. "The number's on there."

He didn't make a move to accept the card. "Okay."

Ash exhaled hard in exasperation. "I shouldn't have to tell you how urgent this is, Van. With that podcast stirring up the public, we need to get ahead of the press on this, and the only way to do that is if you talk to me."

"I understand."

Ash held out the card again.

He waved it away. "I don't need it. Give me an hour, and I'll come in. I want to get this over with."

Ash studied him with narrowed eyes for several moments. Finally, he gave a curt nod. "One hour. Please don't do anything stupid like skip town."

Donovan breathed a sigh of relief. "I'm not going anywhere. I loved Darcy. It was a stupid, toxic, teenage kind of love, but she was my first everything, and I still care about her. I want to know what happened to her more than anyone."

Ash's expression softened. "I know you do. But, speaking as your friend and not the sheriff—"

"I though we weren't friends."

Ash growled at that but continued, "I have to warn you that things are about to get ugly."

"I know."

"One hour, Van."

"I'll be there." He watched Ash leave, his mind racing. Unlike Sheriff Jerry Tennison, Ash had to know he was innocent, so why did agreeing to the interview feel like a step toward the gallows?

Fuck.

He had to go to Sasha, tell her what was happening, and prepare her for the worst. And he should probably contact a lawyer. He never called one when he was interviewed as a dumb eighteen-year-old—a mistake he didn't plan to make a second time.

He had a lot to do in only an hour.

Since Rose was still in her office, he stepped behind the bar himself to retrieve Sasha's lunch. When he straightened from the fridge, he found himself face-to-face with a ghostly pale woman. She had huge dark eyes and hollow cheeks—a walking personification of the word haunted. He stumbled back a step in shock before his busted mind realized it wasn't actually a ghost or another goddamn hallucination.

"Veronica." Her name left him on a hard exhale of relief. "Jesus. Warn a guy before you go sneaking around."

A bit of color returned to her cheeks. "Sorry."

Veronica Martens was an agoraphobic mess of a human, but she had ventured out of her comfort zone to join Redwood Coast Rescue's K9 unit, which he had to give her credit for. Given what she'd survived, it was brave of her even to try. But in the end, it proved to be too much, and she retreated back to her home, emerging only for their group therapy sessions. Really, it was amazing she'd set foot in the Mad Dog at all— even if it was only for therapy while the pub was closed.

"I thought you left." He hadn't seen her since Rose interrupted the session and assumed she'd crept out of the back to avoid all the drama.

"I was going to, but..." She hesitated and hunched in on herself.

"Are you okay?" He started to reach for her shoulder, remembering a half-second too late that it was the wrong move to make. The poor woman had been brutally raped while in the military and didn't trust men. Their group was exposure therapy for her.

She flinched back. "Sorry. I should go." Pulling up the hood of her sweatshirt, she nearly sprinted toward the door.

He hurried around the bar to catch her. "Vee, wait."

To his surprise, she did stop. She drew a breath that shook her thin shoulders, then slowly turned back to him. "I should've mentioned something sooner, but I wasn't sure it was my place. Before she died, Chrissy told me something about—" She broke off and glanced nervously around. She reminded him of a rabbit, constantly searching for threats, ready to run at the first hint of one.

He shook his head, not understanding where she was going with this. "Hang on, you mean Chrissy Jimenez? Our Chrissy from group."

"Yes. She was the closest thing I had to a friend. We bonded over—" Veronica bit down on her trembling lower lip, then drew another deep, fortifying breath. "Over our shared trauma. Right before she died, she was... you know, working the steps. She was trying so hard to get clean so she could hold the military accountable for what happened to us, and she was on number nine—making amends to people she'd wronged. One of those people, she said, was you."

"But she never wronged me."

"She said you didn't know about it." Her gaze lifted briefly to the blank television, and suddenly, he understood.

He sank down onto one of the bar stools, stunned. "Chrissy was at the party on Hidden Beach."

Veronica nodded.

"Holy shit." He hadn't known Chrissy back then. She'd been new in town, having transferred to Redwood Coast High School just a few months before. He didn't meet her until much later, after they'd both returned home broken from their military experiences. "She knew something about what happened to Darcy. That's why she thought she had to make amends."

Another nod.

He jumped off the stool so fast it tipped over. "Did she tell you what she saw?"

"I'm sorry." Veronica shook her head and retreated to the door. "I don't know what good this information does now, but Chrissy was deeply sorry for hurting you by not speaking up back then. I just thought you should know."

chapter
eighteen

"THIS IS REALLY GOOD," Sasha said and took another bite of the teriyaki bowl. "Like, Michelin-starred restaurant good. Where did you learn to cook?"

Donovan raised a shoulder in a half-hearted shrug. "Mostly Mom. She loved her kitchen."

She speared a piece of broccoli. "That was one of the first things Anna said to me after the fire—how much she'd loved her kitchen. I've never had an attachment to mine, but if you keep cooking meals like this in it, I might—" She broke off and poked him with the handle of her fork. "Earth to Donovan."

"Sorry." He put the lid back on his bowl and returned it to the bag. As much as he loved their lunches together, his stomach was too tied up in knots to eat.

Her smile faded. "What's wrong?"

All right. No putting it off any longer. "Ash wants me to go in for questioning regarding Darcy."

Sasha sucked in a deep breath, then pushed back her shoulders like she was preparing for a fight. "We knew this was coming."

"There's more."

"That sounds ominous."

"I was over at the Mad Dog for group when Ash came in to request an interview. After he left, Veronica approached me and said something that..." He trailed off because he still couldn't wrap his mind around it.

"Okay, Donovan. Now you're scaring me."

"Sorry, angel. I don't mean to. The news just knocked me for a loop and I'm still processing it."

"News about Darcy?"

"And Chrissy Jimenez."

"What?"

"Chrissy was at the party that night. I think she witnessed what happened to Darcy, but she was too afraid to say anything at the time. She was going to, though. That's what Veronica told me. Chrissy was at the making amends part of the 12-step program and she was going to come forward."

"But then she died."

He nodded. "All this time, we've been thinking it was a tragic accident. That her addiction got the best of her. But her death is too convenient to be a coincidence."

Sasha's eyes widened, and she set down her fork with a clatter. "Are you saying that someone killed Chrissy to keep her from talking about what she saw?"

"It's possibile, right? I'm not just grasping at straws here?"

"More than possible. Donovan, this is huge."

"But do I tell Ash about all this? I don't have any evidence other than Veronica's hear-say. Can I trust him to look into this?"

"Ash is a good man, and I know he'll listen. But," she added after a beat, "I also know you think my opinion is clouded by the crush I had on him. So, what does your intuition say?"

Donovan turned his gaze inward and took stock. His intuition told him that Ash was a good cop, but it also said there was something deeply wrong with the whole situation. The web of lies surrounding Darcy's—and now Chrissy's—deaths kept getting more tangled and he was starting to suspect a cover-up.

"I want to believe that Ash is on the level, that he'll do the right thing. But I can't take any chances. This is too important and it's all too murky, too... complicated. Ash does not like gray areas." And he couldn't bring himself to trust Ash completely—not when the stakes were this high. He needed to find proof before he could come forward with any of this information. "I feel like we're missing something big, something important."

"So, what are you going to do?"

"I don't know yet," Donovan said. "But I do know one thing. I need to find out what happened to Chrissy. If she was killed because she was going to talk, then we need to find who did it—because that person will clear me of Darcy's murder."

"Then let's do it." She stood and gathered the remains of her lunch.

"Don't you have patients to see?"

"I was going to surprise you and take the afternoon off." She gave a sheepish smile and shrugged. "So... surprise!"

He caught her around the waist and pulled her down onto his lap. "Accompanying me to an interrogation was probably not the afternoon you had planned for us, was it?"

"No, I had sexier things in mind." She looped her arms around his neck and kissed him. "But that can wait. Let's go clear your name first."

As they left the clinic, a woman with sleek blond hair and glasses leaped from a nondescript sedan parked near his Jeep. The plate was from out of state, indicating a rental. "Mr. Scott, could I have a moment of your time? I'm Alexis Summers with the Cold Truth podcast—"

Donovan's shoulders tightened, but he didn't turn toward

the woman's voice. He put a hand on the small of Sasha's back and guided her toward her car.

"We heard a body's been discovered that could potentially be Darcy's and—"

"I have nothing to say."

"Seems like an innocent man would have a lot to say."

"No comment."

"Don't you want your side of the story told?"

"Nope."

Alexis grabbed for Sasha's arm.

Donovan growled and swung Sasha out of the way, planting himself between the two women as a shield. "I said no comment."

Alexis was undeterred. She stood on her toes to address Sasha over his shoulder. "Dr. LeBlanc! Do you know what he's been accused of?"

"Leave. Now." His jaw was clenched so tightly he couldn't get out more than those two clipped words.

Sasha laid a soothing hand on his arm and stepped from behind him. She faced the podcaster and gave her best customer service smile—the one that said you're-a-fucking-idiot-but-I-have-to-be-nice—and he fell even more madly in love with her for it.

"Yes, I'm well aware of the accusations," she said. "I also know he didn't do it, and you can quote me on that. He doesn't owe you or anyone an explanation. Now leave us alone before I call the police. This is private property."

Alexis backed away, throwing her hands up in a gesture of surrender. "Fine, but just remember, Mr. Scott, the truth always comes out in the end."

Donovan watched her go, his hands trembling with anger and the afterburn of adrenaline. He took a deep, steadying breath and turned to face Sasha, who was staring up at him with a mixture of concern and admiration. She believed him, and that was all he needed to know.

He pulled her into his arms and lowered his forehead to hers. "I love you."

She froze, going rigid in his arms.

Shit, too soon. He realized it the moment the words left his mouth and wished he could call them back. He didn't want her to feel obligated to say them before she was ready.

"Donovan..." She backed away, and her gaze darted around the parking lot, looking everywhere but at him.

A pit opened in his stomach. "I know. I shouldn't have said that, but it kinda feels like I'm on death row about to take that final march, so I wanted you to know. Just in case this goes very wrong."

"Don't say that." She groaned and squeezed her eyes shut. "And I do have feelings for you, but it's—I don't know if it's—I'm not ready to—" She broke off like she couldn't figure out how to continue.

"Hey, angel." He hooked a finger under her chin and lifted, waiting until she opened her eyes before he spoke again. "It's okay." He brushed his thumb across her cheekbone and leaned in to press a gentle kiss to her forehead. "We don't have to put a label on anything right now. Let's just take things one day at a time, yeah?"

She nodded, her relief palpable. "We should go. You don't want to be late to meet Ash."

"Yeah," he said on a hard exhale and took a second to fortify himself. "Okay. Let's get this over with."

episode 6: darcy's last words

Welcome back, Truth Seekers. I'm your host, Alexis Summers, and today, we'll read an excerpt from Darcy Cantrell's diary, which sheds some light on her relationship with Donovan and her plans for the future.

> *Oct 26, 2007*
>
> *Van's leaving. He signed up to join the Marines. He's going to boot camp right after graduation.*
>
> *I HATE HIM!*
>
> *This wasn't the plan! We're supposed to escape together! But the fucker is leaving me here in this shitty little town to rot. He said it's only for a little while. He said he'd come back for me after boot camp, and we can get married and then I can go wherever he gets stationed. He'll get me a ring tonight to prove he's serious.*

But then what?

That doesn't sound like an escape to me. That sounds like the same trap both of our moms fell into. Marry young. Pop out a kid we don't really want. Struggle for money our whole lives until he starts drinking every night (he already drinks too much) and we end up in some shitty trailer park in the middle of fucking nowhere, working back-breaking, minimum-wage jobs to barely pay the bills. I don't think Van would ever hit me, but I bet both of our moms thought the same thing when they got married.

Whatever.

I don't need him.

I have $1500 saved and made another $80 in tips tonight. Winter will be slow at the diner, but I can make up for it at the truck stop, and if I stay here and work full-time through tourist season, I'll have enough money to go anywhere by the end of summer.

Goodbye, Cali-fucking-fornia!

I'm thinking New York City. I could get lost there, and nobody will ever find me. I'll become someone else. Someone happy. I really just don't want to be me anymore.

Okay, I've made up my mind. I'm going to break up with Van tonight at the bonfire. I *don't want to go, but it will be worth it to shoot him down in front of all those stupid kids from school he thinks are his friends.*

I'll hurt him before he can hurt me.

PS - Van just called. He's on his way to get me. He said he got a family ring from his mom. It was his grandma's or some shit. And now I'm having second thoughts. I hate him for ruining all of our plans, but he's going to give me his grandma's ring! How could I not still love him, too?

PPS- He's here. I might rip this out and burn it when I get back. Or maybe I'll just leave tonight and never return. We'll see what happens.

Could this prove that Darcy ran away? Or could it be a clue to something more sinister? We know that Donovan Scott was the last person seen with her before she disappeared. And now, with this diary entry, we have reason to believe that Darcy may have been planning to break up with him and leave town on her own. We also know from the interrogation recording that Darcy really did go through with the breakup at the bonfire, and Donovan admitted he was angry at her. Could Donovan have been jealous of Darcy's plans to leave without him? Could his motive have been to prevent her from leaving?

Furthermore, Donovan was uncooperative during his initial questioning with Sheriff Jerry during the search of his home. Remember, he lied about his whereabouts on the night of her disappearance and seemed evasive when asked about his relationship with her. While this all points to him as a suspect, some could argue that he was just a scared teenager who had a history of bad encounters with the sheriff. We must remember that to this day, he has not been charged with a crime and is innocent until proven guilty.

It's all speculation at this point, but one thing is for sure: Darcy's last words, as recorded in her diary, paint a picture of a young woman who was unhappy with her life and desperate for a change. Did she finally make that change on the night she disappeared? Or did something more sinister happen to her?

And that's it for today's episode of Cold Truth. We explored the last words of Darcy Cantrell, and while we can't say for certain what happened to her, it's clear that her relationship with Donovan and her desire to escape played a big role in her final moments. But the question remains: is Donovan Scott guilty or not? Some believe that Sheriff Jerry may have focused too much on Donovan and missed other potential leads. We'll explore that and more in our final episode.

Stay curious, Truth Seekers, and stay safe. See you next time!

chapter
nineteen

THE LAWYER WAS ALREADY WAITING in the parking lot beside the sheriff's department. He walked over as Donovan parked and stretched out a hand. "Donovan Scott? I'm Callum Holden. I believe you spoke with my secretary about needing representation."

"Yeah." He climbed out of his Jeep and accepted the strong handshake. "I know it's short notice. Thanks for coming." When Sasha climbed out of her car moments later and joined them, he placed a possessive hand on her back. "This is Sasha. We can talk freely in front of her."

"Good to know. Hi, Sasha." Holden smiled warmly at her, but it wasn't warm enough to spark off the possessive beast living in Donovan's chest. He didn't feel the need to mark his territory because Holden didn't come off as a threat.

The lawyer had sandy blond hair swept back from an open face that inspired honesty. His suit was nice but a little rumpled, like he'd worn it for one too many days in a row. He kind of reminded Donovan of Winston, Zak and Anna's goofy Golden Retriever, but his reputation as a defense lawyer was more like that of a pit bull. He was mean and persistent and exactly the kind of man Donovan wanted in his corner.

Holden looked over at the blocky building that served as the main office of the Lost County Sheriff's Department and gave a little wince. "I would've liked more time to prep beforehand, but I reviewed the basics before coming over. We got this. I'm good at winging it." He pulled a notebook from the bag on his shoulder and grabbed the pen tucked behind his ear. "So, let me get some things straight before we walk in there. I understand that you're being questioned about the disappearance of your ex-girlfriend."

"Yeah. I've been their only suspect since it happened."

"So why are they dragging you in now? It's been... what? Fifteen years?"

"This isn't the first time they've interviewed me. I was brought in twice for questioning back when Darcy disappeared. I was eighteen and scared and stupid and never asked for a lawyer."

"Okay. I'll see about getting hold of those interviews. Now, I know this is a difficult and stressful situation, but I want to assure you that I'm going to do everything I can to protect your rights and defend you against any charges that may be brought."

"I hope it doesn't come to that."

Sasha reached for his hand and gave it a reassuring squeeze. "You probably hear this all the time, Mr. Holden, but he's innocent."

"Oh, please, just Cal." He glanced back and forth between them, then looked at their tightly joined hands. He nodded, a smile kicking up the corner of his mouth. "You're right. I do hear it all the time, but I don't always believe it. This time? I do. It's a nice change of pace." He went back to making notes. "Do you know what kind of questions they're going to ask?"

Donovan shrugged. "Not really. Ash just said he wants to talk to me about what happened. He said it's routine."

Cal's eyebrows winged up. "You personally know the sheriff?"

"We were friends in high school."

"Okay. Yeah, we can work with that. Before we go in, a few more things." His whole demeanor suddenly changed like he'd flipped on the switch in his brain labeled work, and Donovan saw a glimpse of that pit bull. "Remember your Miranda rights—you have the right to remain silent and the right to an attorney. If you don't feel comfortable answering a question, or if you need time to think about your answer, you can say that you want to speak to me first."

"Got it."

"You want to be honest and straightforward but don't give away any information that could be used against you. It's important to be calm, clear, and consistent in your answers."

"I can do that."

"If they try to pressure you or intimidate you, we're out. You have the right to be treated fairly and respectfully, and I'll make sure that happens."

Sasha exhaled a deep breath. "Thank you for that, Cal. He needed someone other than me in his corner."

"It's my job." Cal checked the time on his phone. "And now we'd better head in."

"Oh, God." Sasha turned into his arms and hugged him tightly around the waist like she didn't want to let him go. "I'll be waiting right here for you."

He wrapped his arms around her and buried his face in her hair, drawing strength from her conviction in his innocence. He wanted to tell her he loved her again but kept his mouth shut and instead kissed her lightly before stepping back.

He faced his lawyer and squared his shoulders. "Let's go."

Ash was surprised to see the lawyer. He hid it, but Donovan knew him well enough to see the flash of shock as Cal introduced himself.

"I appreciate you coming," Ash said and waved a hand at the table between them. "Please, have a seat. I'll try to make this as quick and painless as possible."

"Isn't it a bit unconventional to have the sheriff handling this interview by himself?" Cal said in a light, conversational tone as he pulled out a chair and sat.

It's because Ash is a control freak. But Donovan didn't say that out loud. He didn't figure it would help his case to piss off the sheriff right from the jump.

"My deputies are all busy in other parts of the county dealing with the fire," Ash said evenly.

"Hm." Cal produced a small digital recorder from his briefcase and set it on the table. "I'll be recording this, too, if you don't mind. Or even if you do mind."

"That's fine. This is just a routine follow-up to clarify a few things." Ash pulled out the chair across from them and sat. He started the official recorder and quickly listed off the date, time, and names of everyone present. "Okay, let's start at the beginning: the party on Hidden Beach on the night of October 26, 2007. Tell me about that night."

"You should know, Ash. You were there."

"I want to hear it in your own words. For the record."

Donovan drew a breath and rehashed it all—the ongoing fight with Darcy about him joining the Marines; her dismissal of his marriage proposal; the blow-up fight at the party, where she slapped him before taking off into the woods; his unsuccessful attempt to find her; his stop at the gas station before going home.

Seemed like, after fifteen years, it should be easier to talk about, but reliving that night still left a black hole in the center of his chest.

Ash nodded. "Okay. There's one more thing I have to ask about. The blood found in your home, on the floor, and on your bat."

Cal held up a hand. "If Darcy Cantrell was killed in the woods near Hidden Beach, then I don't see how this question is relevant."

"It's relevant if it's the murder weapon," Ash said flatly.

"Except it's already a well-established fact, verified by multiple witnesses, that my client didn't have his baseball bat with him that night."

Ash's lips thinned, and aggravation flashed in his eyes, but none of it seeped into his voice. "Very well. Is there anything you'd like to add?"

Donovan opened his mouth but then glanced at his lawyer. Might be better to run this by him first. "Can you give us a minute?"

Ash grumbled low in his throat but shut off the recorder and left. After a quick conference with Cal, they let him back in, and he restarted the recording.

Cal stood. "Sheriff, my client has potentially pertinent information to the investigation, but he requests his source remain anonymous."

Ash's eyebrows winged up, and there was a whole lot of *"what the hell?"* on his expression before he shuttered it. "Depends on the information."

Donovan spoke up. "The person who told me this doesn't need to be involved. Their identity has nothing to do with the information they provided."

Ash's silence stretched for several uncomfortable moments. "Fine. Go on."

So Donovan told him about the connection between Chrissy Jimenez and Darcy Cantrell.

"Jesus." Ash jabbed the stop button on the recorder and leaned forward, propping his elbows on the table as he assaulted his scalp with both hands. "Van, that's now two women you've been involved with dying under suspicious circumstances, and you were the last person to see both of them alive. You gotta know how that looks."

"I wasn't involved with Chrissy," Donovan said.

"Bullshit. Everyone saw you two circling each other. If she hadn't died, it would've happened eventually, and we both know it."

"No, we decided we were better as friends. Nothing more."

"Did she not come forward in 2007 because she was protecting you?"

Donovan scoffed. "Why would I tell you about this lead now if she had stayed silent for fifteen years to protect me?"

Ash opened his mouth, but Cal cut in. "If you plan on pursuing this line of questioning any further, Sheriff, we're walking out the door."

Ash sighed and leaned back in his seat, locking his hands behind his neck. "Fuck," he said softly after a moment. "I knew there was something off about Chrissy's overdose, but I couldn't put my finger on it, and there was so much else going on at the time with Zak and Anna, Bella and Poppy—I just took it at face value. I should've looked at it closer. Fuck!" he said again with feeling.

"Ash, c'mon, man," Donovan said. "You couldn't have known it had anything to do with a fifteen-year-old missing persons case. Nobody could've. Chrissy was a drug addict, and, unfortunately, addicts overdose all the time. We had no reason to think it was anything else."

Ash shook his head, his shock evident in his usually closed-off expression. "I can't believe she knew what happened to Darcy. All these years, she knew and didn't say."

Donovan couldn't blame him for his consternation. He'd had a similar response when Veronica told him the news. "Yeah, but I bet she said something to her brother. They were tight, and I told you Tiago's been hiding something. You need to talk to him."

"Is it possible she didn't say anything because she was protecting her brother?" Cal suggested.

Ash and Donovan both shook their heads.

"He wasn't at the party," Donovan said. "He was only... what? Thirteen or fourteen at the time?"

"Sounds about right," Ash said. "But as soon as he's back from the fire, I'll bring him in for an interview."

"Well, Sheriff," Cal said. "Is my client still a suspect, or is he free to go?"

Ash scowled at the lawyer for a moment, but then his gaze shifted to Donovan, and the scowl faded. "I've never considered you a suspect. Like I said, this was routine. It had to be done, and now I've crossed you off my list."

Cal smirked, picked up his digital recorder from the table, and clicked it off. "Thanks, Sheriff Rawlings. That soundbite will be immensely helpful in court if you change your mind and decide to charge my client."

Ash's face dropped as he remembered there wasn't only one recording device in the room. The guy really must be exhausted—he wasn't usually one to make sloppy mistakes like that.

Out in the hall, Ash caught Donovan's arm as he passed. "Hey." He nodded toward the lawyer's back. "I'm glad you hired a lawyer this time. If this goes sideways, Cal Holden is the right man to have in your corner."

chapter
twenty

ASH WATCHED Donovan and Cal cross the dispatch center, then pause in the lobby to shake hands. He'd been telling the truth—he was glad Donovan had secured Cal Holden as a defense attorney. Cal was a massive pain in his ass, which meant he was excellent at his job. But he was also honest and always played within the rules of the justice system—bending them sometimes, but never breaking them. Lawyers didn't get much better than that guy.

Ash glanced around the dispatch center, taking in the rows of computers and the scatter of whiteboards. The dispatchers had a row of cubicles where they kept a finger on the pulse of the community, but the rest of the room was dedicated to his deputies. Several large maps of the county and surrounding areas covered the walls. The space was usually buzzing with activity, but, today, it was silent save for the low murmur from the dispatchers in the corner. All of his deputies were in the field, dealing with the fire.

He crossed the lobby and walked down the short hall to his office. On his desk sat the old paper file folder of Darcy's case that he'd dug up from the cold case archives. He grabbed it and the keys to his Tahoe. The former sheriff had been dodging his calls, but he knew where to find the man.

He drove to the golf course north of town, both surprised and disgusted to see the parking lot almost full. There was a fire raging to the south, and smoke hung thick in the air, but Christ forbid the country club types skipped their 18-holes.

He technically belonged to this club. He had a legacy life-time membership since his several times over grandfather, flush with cash from the Gold Rush, had been one of the founding members. But he'd never had the patience for golf. Or for the snooty people who frequented this place.

He badged the guy at the reception desk, but it didn't get him anywhere until he tapped into his inner Karen and demanded to speak to management. As soon as the manager spotted who was causing the ruckus, her entire demeanor shifted from pleasant, placating customer service representa-tive to sycophant yes-woman, and he supposed there were some perks to being a legacy member. He was considered royalty here.

The manager pointed him toward the bar and restaurant overlooking the golf course, and he stalked through the tables, his mood souring with each step as he approached the table closest to the wall of windows. The former sheriff sat there with his son, Jerry Tennison Jr., or JT as he was often called, and Monarch Development CEO, Mark Salas.

The three of them were deep in conversation and didn't notice his approach until he tossed the file down in front of Jerry.

JT flinched at the slap of the file on the table.

Sheriff Jerry looked a little green as he stared down at it like it was a snake coiled to attack.

But not Mark Salas. He simply leaned back in his seat and offered his trademark smug smile. "Sheriff Rawlings. We don't see you around her often enough." He waved a hand at the empty seat at their table. "Care to join us?"

"You," Ash said and shoved a finger in the guy's face. "Are the entitled fuckhead with more money than brains who has been terrorizing my sister for over a year. I wouldn't dine with you even if we were the last two men on earth and you were on the fucking menu. I'd starve first."

Mark's eyebrows lifted in surprise. "It's just business, Sheriff. Nothing personal."

"It feels fucking personal." He turned his back on the asshole and stared at the former sheriff. "We need to talk."

Jerry cleared his throat. "Uh, well, can it wait? I'm in the middle of lunch and—"

"No, it can't wait. It's waited fifteen years." He opened the file and jabbed the picture of Darcy that the news kept flashing every few hours. "She's waited long enough."

JT stood up abruptly, his napkin sliding off his lap and fluttering to the tiled floor. "I, uh, need the restroom. I'll be back."

Ash ignored the little weasel. JT had never had a backbone, and, for a lawyer, he was shit at confrontation. Maybe that was why he'd gone into corporate law.

He pushed Jerry's plate aside and replaced it with the file. "What the hell is this, Jerry? You tested the blood at the crime scene for blood type but not DNA. You didn't test the shoe. You didn't test the blood stain at Donovan's house. What about the bat? Why didn't you take it into evidence? You never even got Donovan's DNA or fingerprints." Both were on file now thanks to Donovan's service in the Marines, and he'd already sent them to the lab to be tested against the scant evidence collected in 2007, but that didn't negate the fact that Jerry hadn't done his job correctly.

The former sheriff's eyes skittered away. "Times were different back then. Policing was different. It didn't seem like a pertinent move at the time since we never had enough to arrest him."

"You could've at least asked during one of the interrogations if he'd provide them."

Jerry scoffed. "That kid was trouble with a capital T and had one massive chip on his shoulder. He wasn't going to provide anything willingly."

"He would've if it cleared his name."

Jerry said nothing.

"Then, today, the lab goes to check all of that evidence out of storage to see what we can still test, and it's just... gone."

"Stuff gets lost all the time, son. It's unfortunate, but it happens. Now, if you'll excuse me—"

Ash slapped a hand on the table, caging him in his seat. "C'mon, Jerry. You taught me everything I know. You're not a sloppy investigator, but this case file is so thin it barely needs a paperclip. So what happened?"

"Nothing happened. I investigated by the book, but without a body, we just never had a case."

"We have a body now." He'd have to be blind to miss the panicked flick of Jerry's gaze toward Mark. He shifted, positioning himself between them. "Why are you looking at him?"

"Sheriff Rawlings," a smooth voice said behind them. "This is hardly the time or the place for an interrogation."

Ash growled and straightened, turning to face the state attorney general. Thomas Parker was in his mid-fifties but still had the trim build of a younger man. His graying hair was always neatly combed back from his sharp, hawk-like features. JT stood directly behind the man with a self-satisfied look on his skinny weasel face.

"Tom, I suspect there's been long-standing corruption in my department, starting with the former sheriff here. I'm well within my purview to question him."

Tom's too-white smile remained genial, even as his eyes

flashed a warning. "Maybe just not at the club, hm? This has always been neutral ground. Your father and grandfathers would come here to settle disputes, not start them."

"This is an investigation, not a dispute."

"If you suspect corruption, my office will be happy to investigate," he said, his voice still smooth as silk. "But this right here? Ash, this is dangerously close to police harassment. You should take a breath and leave before you do or say something you'll regret."

Ash glowered at him for several heavy seconds, then glanced at the former sheriff. Jerry was staring at the picture of Darcy with tiny beads of sweat gathering at his thinning hairline. Ash looked at Mark, who was utterly relaxed back in his seat, still wearing that smug grin.

And, in his gut, he knew he was looking at Darcy's killer.

It explained so much—like why Monarch had been so desperate to get their hands on Rawlings land. The same land where her body was uncovered. Almost as if Mark knew she was there and had wanted to make sure she remained missing.

"I just remembered," Ash said softly and picked up the file. "*You* were at the party that night, weren't you?" He didn't say more, didn't level accusations. He wanted evidence first, but he also wanted Mark to know his days as a free man were numbered.

Mark's grin slipped just a fraction.

It was all the confirmation Ash needed. He smiled at the four men, and he knew it was a predator's smile from their wary expressions. "Have a nice lunch, gentlemen."

chapter
twenty-one

THE NEXT FEW days passed in a slog. As predicted, the media went nuts over the discovery of Darcy's body. The fire mostly kept reporters from flooding into town, but that didn't stop the talking heads on all the big stations from continuously rehashing the case, flashing that mug shot-like school picture of Darcy next to an actual mugshot of Donovan from when he was arrested for a bar fight a few years back.

People in town were looking at him differently. He'd never been welcomed back with open arms, but there had always been a layer of civility in their dislike. Now, many of them were downright hostile toward him. And he couldn't shake the sense that even Sasha was pulling away from him. They continued sleeping together every night, but she was quieter in the evenings than usual.

Who could blame her?

This was all a lot of stress for a fragile new relationship. Maybe he needed to back off, give her some space. He'd been too pushy, too demanding. He'd had a year to come to terms with his feelings for her, but she'd only had a few weeks. Coupled with everything else, it was a lot to deal with. He needed to give her more time, let her think things through.

Yeah, tonight he'd sleep in his own bed. Without her. Goddammit.

When she left for work, he shut Matilda in the laundry room with a kiss on the nose and her air purifier going, then took Spirit home.

The house was too quiet. Too still. He instantly missed the distinct tippy-tapping of Matilda's paws on the hardwood floor. He missed Sasha's favorite perfume—summertime berries with notes of vanilla—that seemed to saturate every soft surface in her house. His place smelled of man and dog and faintly of the wildfire smoke that still hazed the air.

Donovan sat on his couch and looked around. Although his living room had big windows that let in a lot of light, the walls felt like they were closing in on him. He felt trapped.

Even Spirit seemed sad. She wasn't her usual bouncy self. After roaming the house, looking in every room, she settled down by the door with a big sigh.

"You miss the rescue, don't you?"

She turned her puppy dog eyes up to him and gave another sigh.

"Yeah, me too."

They'd spent every free moment at Redwood Coast Rescue, training or running in the agility yard. And now it was all gone, burned to the ground because some asshole decided to light a fire during a drought.

He couldn't imagine how Zak and Anna and the girls felt now, having lost everything.

Some friend he was. He'd been so wrapped up in his own shit that he never even went to see if they needed help with anything.

He popped to his feet and called for Spirit but stalled out halfway down his front porch steps. He didn't even know where Zak and Anna were living right now. With Zak's parents? A hotel? Had they rented a place somewhere? He had to find out before he dropped by for a visit. And should he even be dropping by unannounced, given his current status as persona non grata in town? Probably not.

He glanced back at his house.

Nope, he wasn't going back inside. He continued on to his Jeep. There was a small dog park over by the high school that had a few agility obstacles. He could take Spirit there and run her through a few times.

Even though it was nearing the end of October, it was still warm and dry, without even a sprinkle of rain forecasted. The fire still raged on the horizon. They were going to lose the entire county if it didn't rain soon.

Nobody else was at the park, which he was thankful for. He unloaded Spirit and ran her through the agility course three times before settling into throwing her ball for her.

By the fifth time she brought the ball back and dropped it at his feet, he felt eyes on him. He glanced over his shoulder, hoping it was just his brain injury revving up his paranoia but fearing it was that podcaster coming back to bug him.

It was neither.

Bella stood there, frozen in surprise, with her backpack on her shoulder. She wore a lot of—in his opinion—unflattering make-up, and in the weeks since he last saw her, she'd cut off her blond dreadlocks. Her hair was now a springy cap of dark curls punctuated with shocks of fire-engine red.

She scowled at him. "What are you looking at?"

"Hey, it's a public park, kid." Donovan shrugged and scooped up the ball Spirit dropped at his feet. "I'm just playing with my dog." He nodded toward the high school, just barely visible through a line of trees. "Shouldn't you be in school?"

"School sucks." Bella draped herself over the fence and watched in fuming silence as he threw the ball again.

Spirit took off like a rocket after it and had it back at his feet in seconds.

After a few more throws, Bella said, "She's really... focused."

"Yeah, she loves this ball."

Another beat of mulish silence passed, then the girl blurted, "Anna says I'm not focused enough on school."

"Is it my face?" Donovan wondered out loud and threw the ball again. "Does my face scream, *I wanna hear all about your problems?*"

Like he didn't have enough of his own.

She scoffed. "You're an asshole."

"I've been called worse." He had every intention of ending Spirit's play session and getting the hell away from the girl, but then he thought of Darcy. Maybe if she'd had someone to talk to—an adult in her life that really listened—things would've ended differently for her.

Aw, fuck.

"So it's back to 'Anna' now?" he asked, keeping his tone disinterested. "Not 'Mom'?"

"I don't know," she muttered and climbed up to sit on the fence. "I bet she wishes I was more like one of her dogs. Easy to train, listens to her every word."

Spirit dropped the ball at his feet and stared at it intensely as if daring it to move again. He smirked down at her. "You obviously haven't met my dog. She does what she wants, when she wants, and nobody's gonna tell her different."

"Not even you?"

"She listens to me. Eventually. Grudgingly."

"So you're saying I should listen to Anna?"

"I'm not saying a damn thing, kid. Just telling you about my dog."

She was silent for several seconds, and he hoped maybe that was the end of it. He'd tried. Wasn't his fault she didn't want to listen to him any more than she did her foster parents.

But then Bella hopped down from the fence and walked

toward him. She picked up the ball and gave it a good, hard throw. Spirit flattened herself out and shot across the park, missing the catch by inches.

"I know she's right," Bella said finally. "But I'm no good at school. I'm so far behind everyone my age. They think I'm stupid."

The flash of anger caught him off guard. He threw the ball harder than necessary—not that Spirit minded—then faced the girl. "Who said that? I'll flatten them."

Hope flared in her eyes. "Could you?" Then she groaned and shook her head. "No, I don't need you to rescue me. It's just... the mean girls. Every school has them."

"Hate to tell ya, it's not just schools."

"Oh, so I get to hear their bullshit for the rest of my life? Great."

"Yeah, but it changes. You'll learn not to care what they think."

"I don't care now."

He raised a brow at her.

She shrugged. "I don't."

"Uh-huh." He tugged at one of her short curls. "Are they the reason for this?"

She ducked away and ran a hand over her head. "Hey, you don't know what it's like."

"Nah, I get it, kid. More than you know. I grew up the same way. The outcast, the poor kid, the troublemaker."

She blinked in shock, and some of the hostility drained out of her. "Was your mom evil like mine? I don't mean Anna," she added quickly. "Anna's amazing. Annoying but amazing. I mean my real—" She stopped. "Well, I guess she wasn't even my real mom, was she? I don't know what to call her. Jessica? The woman who raised me? If you could call it raising. Whatever. *She* was evil. She killed my real parents. I know Ky is technically still alive, which is why Zak and Anna can't adopt me, but he's practically brain-dead because of some infection or... I don't know. They don't think he'll wake up. Do you think he'll wake up? If he does, I'll have to go with him, and I don't want to. Yeah, he's my real dad, and I'm sure he's great, but I don't know him. If he doesn't wake up, but he doesn't die, then I'm stuck in foster care until the system forces me out into some transitional group home. I can't leave Poppy. And I don't want to leave Zak and Anna. But we don't have a home anymore, so maybe they want me to leave. Maybe it would be easier for them to take care of Poppy without me around fucking things up with my bad attitude. Do you think I should leave?"

She finally paused to suck in a shaking breath, and Donovan exhaled softly with relief. He practically had whiplash from trying to follow the girl's line of thinking and decided to answer her first question, which was less of a land-mine than the others.

"It wasn't my mom," he said.

She impatiently wiped at her face with her sleeves and the heavy makeup around her eyes smeared. "What?"

"The evil one in my family? It wasn't my mom. My dad was an asshole who dealt with his shitty life choices by drinking himself stupid and beating on his wife and kid."

"Oh." She swallowed hard, but at least she seemed calmer now. "What happened to him?"

"He's dead. He got drunk and fell off his boat."

"Good."

"Yeah. It made life easier for Mom and me."

Bella released an explosive sigh, and her shoulders dropped, heavy with more weight than a teenager should ever have to bear. "See, and I thought getting away from Jessica would make life easier for Poppy and me. Poppy's doing so good. She's thriving. For her, it's like nothing ever happened. Anna and Zak are Mom and Dad, and it's just... like, in her mind, that's how it always was. I don't think she remembers our life before."

"That's good, right? You should want that for her. She doesn't need to remember."

"I know, but... it was just the two of us against the world for so long. I miss that sometimes."

What did he say to that? He was so far out of his league with this conversation. "Don't you think you should be telling Anna this and not me?"

She gave a half-hearted shrug. "You're easier to talk to. You get it. You're like me."

No, he wasn't like her, but she was like Darcy. He saw so many similarities between them it made his heart ache. They had the same scrappy toughness, the same take-no-prisoners attitude. The difference was Darcy never had a chance, while Bella had a strong support system of people who loved her and only wanted the best for her—even if she didn't realize it.

He released a pent-up breath and squeezed the back of his neck to ease the tension creeping up into his busted skull. "All right, kid. Give me your phone."

Her eyes narrowed in suspicion, but she slid the phone from her back pocket and passed it to him.

He tapped in his number and saved it to her contacts before handing it back. "You can call anytime, okay? I'll always answer. But you need to tell Zak and Anna how you're feeling. Tell them about the mean girls at school—everything."

Bella rolled her lip between her teeth. "Are you going to tell them?"

"Only if you don't." He held out a fist. "Deal?"

She sighed in the way only teenagers could, somehow imbuing that single exhale with irritation and *oh-my-God-you're-so-lame.*

But then she rolled her eyes and bumped his fist with hers. "Fine. Deal."

chapter
twenty-two

SASHA SLOWED to a walk near the dog park and breathed a sigh of relief when she spotted exactly who Bella was speaking with.

Donovan.

When Anna called her in a panic saying Bella had left school and she couldn't get a hold of her, and she and Zak couldn't leave the meeting they were in, Sasha had handed off all of her afternoon appointments and jumped in the car to search for the girl. And when she'd pulled into the high school parking lot and saw Bella in the park, talking to a hulking shadow of a man, her heart had nose-dived into her stomach. She'd grabbed her pepper spray from her glovebox and bolted down the path with every intention of going Auntie Bear on the perv.

But it was just Donovan.

Thank God.

As she drew closer, she caught the tail-end of their conversation, and her heart melted. He was such a good man. He didn't see it because he'd never been given the chance to see his worth. The local gossips didn't see it because they didn't want to—it was more fun to gossip about the town's bad boy. And the media only saw a big, tattooed man with hard eyes and a troubled past.

But she saw his heart, and it was pure gold.

And she loved him for it.

God, she'd been so stupid these last few days for silently freaking out about his confession of love and pulling away from him. She'd started worrying that he was like her dad, using her as a rock to anchor against his problems. And what if, like with her dad, she wasn't enough to keep him here? What if his demons got the best of him, too? If she let herself love him, would he eventually take a gun to his head and leave her alone and devastated? She wouldn't survive that grief a second time.

Did she really want to risk that?

Yes.

And no.

Dammit. She should've talked to him and aired her concerns so they could work through them like adults instead of pushing him away and burying herself in work. She'd blame it on the fact she was new to this whole relationship thing. She'd spent so much of her adult life laser-focused on school and then on her job that she'd never had more than a casual fling before him.

She'd have to make it up to him.

She quickly tapped out a text letting Anna know Bella was safe, then opened the gate to the dog park and stepped inside. Spirit dropped her beloved ball and raced over, her tail waving like a happy flag.

Sasha bent to give her a full-body scratch. "Hi, girl. I'm happy to see you, too."

Both Donovan and Bella looked over at her.

Bella made a face. "Mom sent you?"

"You scared her."

"I wasn't running away or anything like that." At Donovan's gentle nudge, the girl rolled her eyes and scooped up her backpack. "I guess... I just need to talk to her. Can you take me to her?"

"Pretty sure Anna would kill me if I didn't." Sasha held open the gate to let Bella out, then added, "Go up to my car. I'll be there in a second."

Neither she nor Donovan spoke again until Bella was too far away to hear.

"Hi," he said softly.

"Hi," she said back.

A hint of a smile curved the edge of his lips as he nodded to the can of bear spray in her hand. "That's some heavy-duty firepower."

"Oh. Yeah, well..." Heat rushed into her cheeks, and she tucked the can into the pocket of her scrubs. "I thought you were a pervert."

His eyes twinkled. "Only for you, angel."

She exhaled a laugh and stepped forward, wrapping her arms around his waist. "Thank you for those things you said to Bella. She needed to hear it from someone impartial."

He pulled her in tight to him. "She reminds me so much of Darcy. I kept thinking if I didn't hear her out, we'd be finding her body in the woods somewhere, and that would ruin Zak."

She pulled away enough to cradle his stubbled cheeks in her hands. "You're a good man, Donovan Scott. A good friend."

He leaned into her touch. "Jesus, Sasha. I've missed you."

"I know." She stood on her toes to kiss him lightly on the lips. "And that's my fault. I was all up in my head and pulling away, and that's not what I want for us. We should talk about everything." She glanced toward Bella's retreating form, then back at him. "Right now, I have to take her to Zak and Anna. They were in arbitration with Monarch's CEO when the school called. It sounds like the company is no longer interested in the land and is trying to get them to drop the countersuits they'd filed. It's weird they'd suddenly lose interest, right? If anything, you'd think they'd be more interested after the fire because they don't have to clear as many trees for the resort."

"Unless they were after the lumber." Donovan's lip curled. "Fucking Mark Salas. He's probably cooking up some other slimeball scheme to get what he wants."

"Ugh, I hope not. Zak and Anna have been through enough." She stepped back from him but didn't release his hand right away. "I need to go back to work after I drop Bella off. I threw all of my afternoon patients at poor Dr. Richards, and he's getting too old for that heavy of a caseload. But can we have dinner later?"

He raised her hand to his lips. "I want nothing more."

She almost said she loved him. Almost blurted it out right there in the dog park, but bit down on her tongue at the last second. They had to talk first.

She released his hand. "I'll see you later."

Up in the parking lot, she found Bella leaning against her car with tears trailing silently down her cheeks.

"Oh, sweetie. What's wrong?" She knew better than to touch the girl—Bella didn't like hugs—so she stepped up to the driver's side and unlocked the car door.

"I don't know what's wrong with me. I just feel so... lost," she said, her voice small.

Sasha leaned against the car and bumped her shoulder to Bella's. "You know, it's okay to feel lost sometimes. But you're not alone, okay? You have your parents and grandparents. Your sister. Me and Donovan and the rest of Redwood Coast Rescue. We all love you very much."

Bella rested her head on Sasha's shoulder. "It's just...everything is so fucked up. Mom and Dad not being able to adopt me. The fire. School. I don't know where I fit in. I feel like a burden."

"You're not a burden," Sasha said firmly. "You're family."

Bella gave her a tentative smile, but Sasha could tell she was still struggling with something. "What's really going on, Bella? You know you can talk to me about anything, right?"

Bella hesitated for a moment before blurting out, "I think I might be gay."

Oh, wow. Sasha's heart skipped a beat. She hadn't been expecting that. "Okay," she said calmly. "It's fine if you are. And if you're worried Zak and Anna will reject you because of it, they'd never. Not in a million years. They love you and they want you to be happy. And you know Zak's sister—your Aunt Zara—is gay and everyone accepts her and loves her just as she is."

"I know. I've talked to her about it some, but I didn't tell her I am. Or think I am. Or whatever. Just pretended I was curious."

"Well, you should tell her. She can help you deal with all the things us straight people can't understand. And you should talk to your parents about it."

"I'm scared," Bella admitted, her voice trembling. "What if they don't accept me because I'm not blood-related like Zara is? What if they think there's something wrong with me? Or I'm, like, sick or something? What if they decide I'm not worth the trouble of keeping?"

Sasha rubbed her back soothingly. "Hey, listen to me. You are not wrong or sick or anything like that. You are perfect just the way you are. And if anyone ever tells you otherwise..." She ventured a guess: "Like the mean girls at school?"

Bella nodded miserably.

"They're the ones who are wrong. And as for your parents, there is no way in hell they'd ever give you up. They are fighting tooth and nail to adopt you."

Bella wiped her tears with the back of her hand. "Thanks, Sasha. You always know what to say."

Sasha smiled at her. "That's what honorary aunts are for. You ready to go see your parents?"

She took a deep breath and nodded. "Yeah. Let's do it."

Sasha slid behind the wheel and Bella climbed into the passenger's seat. Just as she was about to turn on the engine, Spirit came streaking toward the car, barking like crazy.

Bella froze with her seatbelt half buckled. "What's wrong with her?"

"I don't know. I've never heard her make that sound before."

She saw Donovan racing up the path behind the dog. He was waving his arms and shouting something.

She rolled down the window and at first couldn't hear him over Spirit's frantic barks. Then his shouts registered.

"Get out of the car! Out of the car! Bomb!"

Sasha's heart dropped like a rock into the pit of her stomach, and she very slowly unfastened her seatbelt. "Bella. Don't touch anything and get out slowly and carefully."

Bella pushed open her door and slid from the seat—

"No!" Donovan's voice boomed across the lot.

And, too late, as Bella jumped out of the car, Sasha realized what he'd actually been shouting...

Don't get out of the car.

chapter
twenty-three

DONOVAN'S HEART stopped when he saw Bella dive out of the car. He held his breath, waiting for the explosion...

Nothing.

Okay. Bella's seat wasn't rigged.

He grabbed the girl and ushered her over to his Jeep, parked at the far side of the lot. She was gray-faced and shivering so hard her teeth clacked together. "Are you hurt?"

She shook her head. "Is Sasha—did I hurt Sasha? I didn't know."

"It's okay. Sasha's okay."

"I thought you said to get out. Sasha said to get out." She dissolved into sobs, and he didn't have time to comfort her.

He grabbed his bomb kit—you could take the Marine out of EOD, but you could never take EOD out of the man. He'd carried this damn kit with him everywhere since his discharge, and for once, he was grateful for his paranoia.

He still couldn't believe Spirit had caught the scent of the explosives from so far away. The wind had shifted, and she'd stiffened, raising her nose to the air, going from ball-obsessed pet to explosive detection K9 in a heartbeat. She'd cleared the dog park fence in a single bound and raced up the hill toward the parking lot. As he chased her, he saw his Darcy hallucination standing by Sasha's car, smirking at him, and he'd known what was happening even before Spirit signaled on the car.

"I'll get her out," he told Bella. "Keep Spirit here with you and call 911."

The girl was still sobbing, but she nodded and wrapped her arms around Spirit.

Bomb kit in hand, he raced back to Sasha. "You okay, angel?"

"I-I don't know. Am I sitting on a bomb?"

He peered through the window. He could see the pressure plate rigged under the driver's seat and wires leading to something beneath the dash. "Sasha, sweetheart, I need you to stay calm and keep your hands where I can see them. Don't put them on the wheel. We don't want to risk triggering anything. Cross them over your chest and stay as still as possible."

"Oh my God," she breathed. "I am. I'm sitting on a bomb."

"Yes, but I'm going to get you out of there. This was my job for over a decade, remember? And I was damn good at it. The best. You couldn't be in better hands." Except his hands were currently shaking. He closed his fingers into fists at his sides so she wouldn't see.

She nodded, wide-eyed, and he got to work. He spread his tools out on the pavement and carefully opened the door, kneeling to get a better look at the pressure plate. It hadn't detonated when Sasha sat on it, so it must have been rigged to blow when she got up, meaning there had to be a trigger switch somewhere. He had to find that switch first and disable it without jostling the bomb.

Sweat stung his eyes, but his hands were thankfully steady again as he traced his fingers along the wires from the pressure plate. He found the switch on the floor by Sasha's seat near the lever that worked her gas cap—a small button disguised to look like a harmless piece of plastic, but to anyone who knew what they were looking for, it was an unmistakable red flag. When she sat down, the button completed a circuit that sent a signal to arm the detonator. As soon as she tried to leave the seat—boom. It was a simple but effective design.

"Stay still a little longer," he said softly. "Almost done." He exhaled a long and slow breath to calm his hammering heart, then snipped the wires leading to the button. "Okay. Got the trigger. Now for the detonator." He followed the wires from the plate along the edge of the door. They disappeared into the dashboard. "Fuck."

"What?" Sasha said, her face draining of color. "I didn't like the sound of that fuck."

"I thought the detonator was under the dash, but it's up inside. I'll have to dismantle the dashboard to get to it."

"Oh." The word left her in a terrified squeak. Tears fell from her eyes with every blink. "Okay. Insurance should cover that, right?"

Goddammit, she was in shock. He wanted to touch her, comfort her, but knew better. "Hey." He waited until her gaze slid toward him. Her eyes were glassy and showed too much white. "I won't let anything happen to you, angel. Do you trust me?"

"Yes." Her answer came without hesitation.

"Okay. I'm going to walk over to my Jeep, check on Bella, and get my bigger toolbox."

She nodded in a tiny, jerky up-down motion. "Hurry."

At his Jeep, Bella still sat in the backseat in wide-eyed shock, her arms tightly around Spirit's neck. "Almost done," he assured her.

She nodded, but he could tell she hadn't actually heard him. She was miles away.

He returned to Sasha with his toolbox and slid a headlamp onto his forehead as he knelt beside the driver's seat. "I'm going to pry the cover off this side panel. I'll have to get in real close to see what I'm doing, and it's going to be awkward, but don't move. No matter what, don't move."

Again, she gave the tiny, jerky nod that was more with her eyes than her head.

He made short work of the panel and easily found the detonator—a small device about the size of a cell phone, with a series of buttons and switches on the front, nestled deep in the wiring of the car. But, thankfully, not wired into the car. It was one of the most sophisticated detonators he'd ever seen, with multiple fail-safes built in to prevent tampering. It was a testament to the skill of whoever had built it.

One wrong move and he'd lose Sasha forever.

He reached in and gently removed the detonator from its hiding spot. A light started flashing rapidly.

Okay. It didn't like that.

And he had zero interest in waiting around to see what that light meant.

He had to move fast.

He could feel Sasha's eyes on him, watching his every move as he examined the wiring. He could hear the sound of his own breathing, ragged and uneven. He was sweating profusely, but he didn't dare wipe his brow.

This was sophisticated work—master-level bomb-making—but it had been installed fast, because Sasha was only down at the park for ten, fifteen minutes, tops. Which meant the master bomb maker hadn't bothered with all of the fail-safes.

Lucky for him.

Using his wire cutters, he snipped the wires he could tell were the least threatening. Then he moved on to the more dangerous ones, and each snap of a wire breaking sent a thrill of fear through his body. He flashed back to Afghanistan, to the one time he hadn't been the best at his job, and his hand faltered.

No.

Fuck.

He couldn't let his mind wander. He had to focus. Had to breathe. One mistake could cost him his life and the lives of Sasha, Bella, and Spirit. It could damage the high school he graduated from and possibly hurt teachers and students inside.

He could not let that happen. He reached in with his free hand to support his wrist and kept working.

Finally, the last wire fell away, and the detonator stopped flashing just as the first wail of a police siren tore through the air.

Donovan let out a deep sigh of relief, checked to make sure there were no other triggers he may have missed, and then pulled himself out from under the dashboard. He turned to Sasha, who was still sitting rigidly in her seat, weeping in silent, shuddering gasps.

He reached out and took her freezing hand in his. "It's over, angel. You're safe now." He helped her from the seat and caught her when her legs gave out.

Sasha leaned into him and wrapped her arms around him, burying her face in his chest. He felt each tremble that jolted through her and each frantic beat of her heart. He ran a hand down her spine. "Shh. You're okay."

"You saved me." Her eyes lifted to his, full of equal parts terror and wonder. "I-I can't believe that just happened. Why would someone want to kill me?"

Donovan's jaw clenched as anger sparked hot inside him. *To hurt me.* He didn't say it out loud. He was afraid she'd pull further away from him if he gave that thought voice. Not that he'd blame her if she did. Hell, maybe she should stay far away from him because obviously someone in town was pissed about him and Darcy and that fucking podcast. Someone dangerous thought he got away with murder and wanted to hurt him for it.

Over Sasha's head, he watched as Ash's Tahoe slammed to a halt, blocking all other cars from entering the parking lot. More deputy vehicles filed in behind the sheriff, clogging the street and setting up barricades around the school.

It was going to be absolute chaos soon, with parents showing up, rightfully demanding to see their kids. If he had kids, he would chew through the police barricades and tear down walls with his bare hands if he thought they were trapped and in danger.

Jesus. First, this fucker set fire to a dog rescue, and now he put a bomb near innocent kids.

Whoever did this was going to pay.

Ash ran over to them, and he looked even more frazzled than he had during the interrogation days before. He had a coffee stain on his button-up shirt, his hair and beard were both a wild mess, and his eyes were crazed with fear. "Bella?" he demanded.

Donovan lifted his chin toward his Jeep. "Spirit's with her."

Ash started in that direction but stopped short. "The device?"

"Disarmed."

Ash raced toward his niece, cursing in a creative string that Donovan would've found hilarious if his own fear hadn't suddenly beat out the adrenaline and overwhelmed him. He tightened his grip around Sasha and pressed his face into her hair, blinking hard to keep back the tears burning in his eyes.

"It's okay," he repeated over and over, as much to assure himself as her.

He felt a hand on his shoulder and looked up to see Ash and Bella. The sheriff held his niece tucked securely under one arm and held his free hand out for a handshake. His expression was a mixture of gratitude, terror, and rage. "Thank you, Van."

Donovan nodded, not trusting himself to speak, and accepted the handshake.

"It's not safe to stay here," Ash said and hugged Bella to his side. "Can you follow me down to the station and give a statement?"

Again, he could only nod. He'd go anywhere if it meant getting Sasha as far away from the bomb as possible. He returned his attention to her and rubbed soothing circles on her back.

"Hey, angel. Did you hear Ash? We need to get out of here," he said gently. "Can you walk?"

Sasha nodded, still holding onto him tightly. He helped her to her feet and led her over to his Jeep. Spirit was still sitting in the back and licked Sasha's cheek as she settled into the passenger seat.

Donovan climbed behind the wheel and waited for Ash to bundle Bella into his vehicle before pulling out of the parking lot. As they drove away, the chaos of the scene faded into the background, and he focused on Sasha. He reached over and took her hand, lacing their fingers together. She was still trembling, and her eyes were wide and unseeing. He knew the fear and adrenaline would linger long after the danger was over.

"It's okay," he murmured. "You're safe now. We're going to the sheriff's office, and you can give your statement. Then, I'll take you home. You can take a hot shower, crawl into bed, and rest. I'll stay with you all night."

"Thank you," she whispered, her voice hoarse from crying. "If you and Spirit weren't there…"

He didn't even want to consider that. "I'll always be there for you, angel. Always."

They drove the rest of the way in silence, Sasha's hand gripping his tightly.

When they arrived at the sheriff's department, he escorted her inside and stayed close as she recounted the events to a deputy in one of the interrogation rooms. Afterwards, Ash met them in the front lobby. It was a well-lit area with blown-up photos of local scenery on the walls and a large wooden desk at the center. The department's receptionist was busily typing on her computer, not paying them any attention except to offer a distracted smile as the sheriff walked by. Ash had changed his shirt into a wrinkled gray button-up and finger-combed his hair and beard, but he still looked exhausted.

"How's Bella?" Sasha asked.

"Shaken, but Zak and Anna are with her in my office now. They're shaken, too. And pissed. So am I." His fists curled at his sides. "This is the second attack on my family in less than a month."

"Do you have any leads?"

Ash nodded and looked at Donovan. "It's Tiago. You were right. I tried to track him down, but he never reported to the fireline like he was supposed to. I did talk to his captain, and Redwood Coast Rescue isn't the first time he conveniently arrived on the scene of a fire before everyone else."

"So he's a classic firebug, setting fires to be a hero." Donovan thought back to the figure standing in the flames. "Except RWCR broke that pattern. He didn't save anyone there. He just watched it burn."

Ash pressed his lips together in a grim line. "Seems like his only goal now is destruction. He's gone AWOL, and he took a shit-ton of explosive material with him when he left."

"Does he have explosives training?"

Ash nodded. "He's part of their hazardous materials team."

"That explains the sophistication of the set-up in Sasha's car. It wasn't done by an amateur. There were all kinds of fail-safes in place. He didn't have time to activate them all, but with his training, he'd have the expertise to create something like that."

"We know he's responsible for the arson at RWCR but don't yet have any definitive proof he planted the bomb," Ash said. "The bomb squad has taken it into evidence, and the explosives in it are a match to some that he took. We're dusting it for fingerprints."

"But..." Sasha shook her head. "Why would he plant it in *my* car? I barely know him. Only met him that one time."

Ash didn't answer and simply stared at Donovan, passing him the conversational ball.

Yeah, okay, that was fair. This was his mess, after all.

He turned her toward him and rubbed his hands up and down her arms. "It's because of me, angel. To hurt me. For some reason, I think Tiago blames me for his sister's death, and this is him getting revenge."

"You were the last person to see her alive," Ash said. "It's an easy conclusion to jump to from the outside."

Sasha broke out of his arms and paced a few steps down toward the front door, then swung back. "This is all... too much. I-I really need to go home and sleep."

"Okay, I'll take you."

She held up her hands and backed up a step, widening the distance between them. "No. Please. I need—to not be near you right now. Ash, would you mind driving me?"

"No, of course not. Let me grab my keys." He walked toward the hall to the left of the lobby and disappeared through the door at the end marked with his name.

Donovan waited until they were alone again before he spoke. "I didn't hurt Chrissy."

Sasha closed her eyes. One of the deputies had brought her a fleece blanket during questioning, and she now hugged it tighter around her. "You say that a lot. You didn't hurt Darcy. You didn't hurt Chrissy..."

"Because I didn't."

She opened her eyes and met his gaze for an instant before focusing on the floor between them. "I... want to believe you."

"But?" he prompted because he heard the unspoken one at the end of her sentence.

"I've been listening to the podcast."

Fuck. He should've known curiosity would get the better of her. "It doesn't paint a flattering picture of me. Or, for that matter, of Darcy."

"I know."

"It's twisting the truth for ratings."

"Probably. But..." She released her breath in a sigh that moved her shoulders. "I don't know how I feel about it, Donovan."

His heart cracked right down the middle. He clutched his chest, wondering for an instant if he was going to keel over right there in the lobby. "You don't believe me anymore."

"It's not that. It's..." She waved a hand around them, encompassing the lobby, the hall of offices to the left of them, and the dispatch center to the right. "All of this. Even if you are innocent, I don't know if I can do this. I don't know if I can live with this constant shadow of suspicion and threat of danger. Are we going to end up in one of these interrogation rooms every few days for the rest of our lives? Are they going to pull you in for questioning every time a girl goes missing or a body turns up?"

He dropped his arms helplessly to his side. "We could leave. We don't have to stay here."

"But this is my home. All of my friends are here. My patients. My life." She stopped pacing and met his gaze. "I'm not walking away from this relationship for good, okay? I just... this is a lot. I need a second to breathe and—"

"What, make a plan?" His laugh was bitter. "You can't plan love or life. A checklist isn't going to keep you from getting hurt or experiencing grief again. A list won't bring your dad back, Sasha."

She flinched. "That was low."

He knew it. And he didn't care because he was in pain, bleeding out from the deep cuts each of her truthful words had inflicted.

But he also knew he couldn't let her go. Not yet. Not without a fight. "I'm sorry," he said, taking a step closer to her. "I didn't mean that. I'm scared. Scared of losing you. Scared of losing everything."

"Me, too," she whispered but still backed toward the door. "But I think... for now, we need some time apart."

His heart sank. Time apart? Was this the beginning of the end? "How much time?"

"I don't know yet."

Donovan watched her push through the door and disappear into the haze of smoke outside. His heart was like a lead weight in his chest, crushing his stomach into knots and weighing down his lungs so he couldn't draw a full breath. He wanted to run after her and take back everything he'd said in the last five minutes, to hold her close and beg for her forgiveness, but he knew that wouldn't change anything.

He'd defused the bomb, but the damage had already been done.

He sagged against the wall and closed his eyes, forcing himself to take a deep breath before he passed out from oxygen deprivation. He needed to find a way to clear his name and prove to Sasha that he was innocent. He couldn't blame her for her doubt or for wanting distance after today, but he couldn't lose her— not when she was the best thing he'd ever had in his life.

Footsteps approached from the direction of Ash's office, and he opened his eyes to find not only Ash but also Zak standing there. He could still see the boys in the two men—the brothers he'd once loved like family. He missed them.

Zak's expression was full of sympathy. "I'm sorry, man. That was rough."

Donovan rubbed a hand over his face, pushing away the tears he refused to cry. "Seeing that doubt in her eyes was like a knife slicing me open."

Zak nodded. "I get it. Anna looked at me like that once, and it felt like a death blow. I didn't think we'd recover from it, but we did. And so will you and Sasha."

"Not unless I can clear my name."

They both looked at Ash.

He held up his hands in protest but then dropped them back to his sides—almost like the move had been an involuntary reaction. He gave a long-suffering sigh. "Yeah, I'll help you clear your name, and I know exactly where to start. I have to take Sasha home, and you should take your dog home," he said to Donovan. "But then how about a ride-along?"

Zak grinned. "Will I get to kick some ass with my shiny leg?"

"No," Ash said and turned away. "You both will be there as witnesses only."

"You could deputize us—"

"Fuck, no," Ash said with feeling.

part three
extinguish

"For what can be more noble than to slay oneself? Not literally. Not with a blade in the guts. But to extinguish the selfish self within, that part which looks only to its own preservation, to save its own skin. "

Steven Pressfield

episode 7: questioning the investigation

Hey there, Truth Seekers! Welcome back to Cold Truth. In our last episode, we read an excerpt from Darcy's diary, which shed some light on her state of mind leading up to her disappearance. Today, we'll be discussing the investigation and some of the criticisms that have been raised about it.

Now, right from the beginning, Sheriff Jerry was pretty focused on Donovan Scott as a suspect, and some critics argue that he didn't explore other leads enough.

What other leads, you ask? Well, there were reports of a suspicious-looking vehicle in the area around the time of Darcy's disappearance. The make and model of the car were never identified, and it's unclear whether it was ever even investigated. Why didn't Sheriff Jerry follow up on that? Could this have been the vehicle used to transport Darcy's body or possibly even used by the abductor to take her? We may never know.

The anonymous phone call that police received, claiming to have information about Darcy's whereabouts, is another lead that was not taken seriously. What information did the caller have, and why did they choose to remain anonymous? Why didn't they ever try to call back? Was this call made by the perpetrator, or was it a genuine attempt to help with the investigation?

There were also reports of a man with a red beard seen in the area around the time of Darcy's disappearance. This man has never been identified, and it's unknown whether he was ever questioned. Could he have been involved, or was he simply a witness? Either way, it seemed like someone should've spoken to him, but for some reason, Sheriff Jerry dismissed this possible suspect early on and instead focused entirely on Donovan.

And what about the crime scene? Critics have pointed out that investigators called off the search of the surrounding woods too soon, and other areas where Darcy could have potentially gone were never searched at all. Instead, all of their efforts focused on the area where her shoe and blood were found.

Now, remember: this case is still open, and it's possible that other leads are being pursued that haven't been made public. When asked about the case, the current sheriff, Ashley Rawlings, was hesitant to comment and only said it was an ongoing investigation that he and his deputies are taking very seriously. He also said that he hasn't ruled out any suspects but that they aren't currently investigating Donovan Scott.

Does the new sheriff believe that the investigation was too narrowly focused on Donovan and that other leads were not pursued as aggressively as they could have been? Sure seems that way.

Donovan did go on to join the Marines and served as an explosive ordnance disposal tech for thirteen years until he was medically retired in 2021 following a traumatic brain injury. His military record was spotless, but unfortunately, he picked up his old troublemaking ways as soon as he returned home. In 2022, he was charged with assault for attacking a man at a bar in Steam Valley. He was court-ordered to attend therapy for anger management, PTSD, and substance abuse. However, it's important to note that erratic behavior isn't uncommon with TBIs and does not necessarily reflect on who he was as a teenager. It is possible that Donovan was wrongly accused, and if that's the case, I can't imagine what this all has been like for him.

He declined to be interviewed for this podcast.

So, what do you think? Do you believe Donovan is guilty, or do you think the investigation was too narrow in its focus? Who else could be a potential suspect? There are still many unanswered questions surrounding the disappearance of Darcy Cantrell, and while we may never know exactly what happened to her that night, we can honor her memory by making sure she's not just a forgotten cold case. Darcy doesn't have any family left. Her father died of cancer in 2011, never knowing what happened to her. So it's up to us as truth seekers to continue the search and, hopefully, find justice for her.

And with that, we come to the end of Cold Truth's investigation into the disappearance of Darcy Megan Cantrell, but please remember that there are countless other cases like Darcy's, where victims have been left without justice, and families left without closure. It's important to continue to raise awareness and advocate for those who can no longer speak for themselves.

Thank you for listening to Cold Truth. I'm Alexis Summers reminding you to stay curious, stay safe, and keep seeking the truth.

chapter
twenty-four

"CAN I just say I strongly advise against this," Cal Holden said from the backseat of Ash's Tahoe.

"Noted," Ash, Donovan, and Zak all said at the same time.

"And ignored," Zak added cheerfully.

Cal raised his eyes to the ceiling as if asking a higher power for patience. "Then why am I even here?"

"Because I hired you to cover my ass," Donovan said. "So, cover it."

Cal winced. "You know I'm not that kind of guy, right? No offense. I like you, and you're okay looking and all for a dude, but I'm all about the ladies."

Zak grinned over his shoulder from the passenger seat. "And he's a smart-ass. Good. You'll fit right in, Holden."

"Not sure I want to fit in with you guys," Cal muttered and sank back in his seat as the Tahoe stopped in front of Monarch Development Corp's main office. "People around you tend to disappear. Or get shot. Or firebombed. I like my bacon extra-crispy, not my skin."

Ash grumbled low in his throat and shut off the car. "Just what I need, more smart-asses in my life."

Zak chuckled. "Ignore the bear in the driver's seat. He forgot to hibernate, and he's grouchy."

Ash pushed open his door. "Remember, you are not deputies. You are here solely as witnesses."

"Uh," Cal said and held up a finger in the universal gesture of hold on a second. "If I'm here to cover asses, I'd recommend you deputize them."

"Fuck," Ash muttered. Then, "Fine. You're all deputies now. Happy?"

Zak pumped a fist in the air and followed him to the sidewalk.

Donovan didn't move. He couldn't seem to make his limbs work, couldn't grasp the door and shove it open.

"You good?" Cal asked and squeezed his shoulder.

He shook his head. "What if this doesn't work? I've lived with this hanging over my head for so long... I can't imagine it finally being over."

"Hey, Ash Rawlings is a man with a plan, and he never fails. It's fucking annoying. All the defense attorneys I know shudder in fear when they see his name on a police report because he is a solid cop with a superior arrest record and a reputation for dotting all of his Is and crossing all of his Ts. And jokes aside, as your lawyer, I'm here to tell you this will work. Your name is about to be cleared, man."

Donovan sucked in a breath and forced his hand to move from his knee to the door handle.

"That's the spirit," Cal said.

The three of them spread out and followed Ash into the building like a defensive line. The secretary's smile fell away when she spotted them approaching, and she grabbed the receiver of her desk phone.

Ash placed a hand over hers. "No need to call security, ma'am." He produced a rolled stack of papers from his back pocket and handed them to her. "I have a search warrant for Mark Salas's office."

The secretary's eyes widened as she scanned the warrant. "I-I'll call Mr. Salas and let him know."

"I'd appreciate if you didn't," Ash said and took the warrant back from her. "We'll be heading up now."

The elevator ride up to the top floor was silent, the tension in the small space palpable. Donovan was surprised the others couldn't hear his heart trying to beat out of his chest. This was it. This was the moment he had been waiting for, the moment that would clear his name and free him from years of unjust suspicion.

As they stepped off the elevator, they were met with a sleek, modern office space that seemed to go on for miles. Glass walls separated various departments, and people in suits bustled around. Donovan followed Ash, Zak, and Cal as they made their way to Salas's office.

Ash knocked briskly on the door, then pushed it open before anyone could answer. Mark was sitting at his desk, his eyes glued to his computer screen. He looked up at the intrusion, his eyebrows raised in surprise. "What the hell is this?"

Ash ignored the question. He simply held up the search warrant and tossed a pair of latex gloves at Zak. "Toss the place."

"With pleasure," Zak said, his smile all teeth as he pulled the gloves on. He moved around the office, rifling through drawers and files.

Mark half-rose from his desk. "You have no right— "

"We have a search warrant, Mr. Salas," Ash said. "And a lawyer here to verify we do everything by the book."

Mark's eyes flicked to Cal, then shifted to Donovan, who stood at the back of the group. "And what's the basis for this search?"

Ash stepped forward, his face set in a grim line. "We have

reason to believe that you were involved in the murder of Darcy Cantrell. It's all there in the warrant. Feel free to read it."

Mark sat back down and reached for his phone. "Fine. Go ahead and search." His smirk faded into a scowl as he dialed. "But I'm calling my lawyer."

"Yeah, get JT up here," Ash said and pulled another pair of gloves from the pocket of his Lost County Sheriff's Department jacket. "It will save me the trouble of tracking him down to arrest him."

Mark shook his head, a small smile playing at the corners of his lips. "I'm afraid you're mistaken, Sheriff. I had nothing to do with Darcy's murder."

Donovan suddenly had a flash of the younger Mark wearing sunglasses, even though it was dark, and layered polos —light blue and pink—with the collars popped and a tie knotted loosely around his neck. He'd been drunk and obnoxious and had flipped a card table full of red Solo cups after losing a round of beer pong. He'd hit on Darcy as she stormed away. She'd ignored him...

...and then he'd followed her into the woods.

Donovan remembered it so clearly now and played it over in his head like a movie on repeat. He remembered Darcy scowling at the tiny diamond in his grandmother's ring and slapping him when he said she was acting like a bitch. He could almost still feel the sting of the slap on his left cheek. He remembered watching her run off into the woods and seeing Mark follow after her with JT chasing close behind. He remembered bitterly thinking Mark and Darcy deserved each other before turning away and downing his beer.

He stared at Mark across the desk and wanted to put a fist through his conceited face. His fingers curled at his sides. "You followed her. What did you do to her, you bastard?"

Mark's face twisted in anger, and he stood up from his

desk. "I didn't do anything to her. You killed her, you piece of shit trailer trash, and everyone knows it."

"Then why did you follow her?" Donovan pressed, taking a step forward.

"I don't have to answer that," Mark said.

"Well..." Cal said, drawing the word out. "Yeah, technically, you don't. Fifth Amendment and all that. But you're under suspicion for murder, and I try to tell my clients to avoid pleading the fifth when they can. It always makes you look guilty."

Mark clenched his jaw, then slowly sat back down at his desk. "Fine. I followed her because she was acting weird. I thought she might be sneaking off to do drugs or something."

"And did you find her doing drugs?" Ash asked.

Mark shook his head. "Nope. I couldn't find her, so I went home."

Donovan's blood started a low boil. "You're lying. Darcy watched her mom die of an overdose. She didn't do drugs."

"But she sold them. And more," Mark added, his greasy smile slithering back into place. "Ah, I see you didn't know she'd been whoring herself at the truck stop when she wasn't spreading her legs for you. She was a slut. You ask me, she got what she deserved."

Donovan felt like he'd been punched in the chest. "She wouldn't..." He trailed off because, as much as it hurt, he heard the ring of truth in Mark's words.

More than anything, Darcy had wanted to escape, but she needed money to do it. How often had she complained that The Grove didn't pay enough? She was so afraid she'd be stuck in Steam Valley forever that she absolutely would have turned to selling drugs or even her body if it meant she could leave sooner.

He squeezed his eyes shut, his heart aching for the girl he'd once loved to distraction. "You killed her." He knew it without a doubt.

Mark chuckled and spread his hands. "Even if I did, you can't prove I was there that night."

"Watch me," Ash said, his voice low and dangerous. "Zak, check his computer. We're looking for any files related to Darcy Cantrell."

"Wait, I have a better idea," Cal said and pulled out his phone. He scrolled for a moment and then grinned like the cat who ate the canary and held up the phone so everyone could see the screen. "Look at that. Someone forgot to set their Facebook to private. And, oops, also forgot to go back and delete all of their embarrassing party pictures. If I'm not mistaken, that douchebag playing beer pong on Hidden Beach on October 26, 2007, is you, Mark. And *that*..." He pinched his fingers on the screen, zooming in on the girl in the background of the photo. "...is Darcy Cantrell."

"So what if I was there? Doesn't mean I killed—" His eyes popped wide as Zak pulled a decorative box off the bookshelf and flipped the lid.

Zak stared down into it for a moment, then looked up, his face grim. "Ash."

Ash crossed to him, looked into the box, and grabbed his handcuffs. "Mark Salas, you're under arrest for the murder of Darcy Cantrell."

Donovan held his breath and crossed the room in three long strides. He didn't want to see what had put that grim horror on his friends' faces, but he knew he'd never find peace if he didn't look.

In the box, under a dirty red canvas shoe, was a handful of photos that had obviously been printed at home by a LaserJet printer. They were sloppily cut and yellowed around the edges, but they clearly showed a girl on her knees, her clothes torn off. Her hands were tied behind her back with the tie

Mark had been wearing that night. One of her eyes was swollen shut, but the other brimmed with tears as she pleaded with the person behind the camera.

Donovan strode across the office, yanked Mark out of his chair, and slammed a fist into his face until he had two black eyes to match the one Darcy sported in the picture. Then he let the asshole drop to his feet and walked away.

"I didn't see that," Cal singsonged and deliberately looked up at the ceiling.

"No?" Zak said, his voice cold. "Because I did. He was clearly resisting arrest and getting violent with a deputy. Right, Ash?"

"That's exactly what I saw," the by-the-book sheriff said without a flicker of hesitation and clicked the handcuffs around Mark's wrists.

"Fuck," Cal muttered. "I knew I'd regret coming here. At least read him his rights."

Donovan ignored them all and shoved through the office door, nearly knocking JT into the wall. When the little shit tried to slink away, he grabbed him by the collar and threw him into the office. Because JT Tennison had been in those photos, too, eagerly participating in the rape and murder of an innocent girl.

"There's the other one," he said through his teeth, then strode away. He took the stairs, not wanting to wait for the elevator, and made it out into the smoke-heavy air before his knees gave out.

He sank to the sidewalk, and that was where Zak and Cal found him minutes later. They didn't say anything, simply picked him up, one man under each of his arms, and carried him to the Tahoe as several other deputy cars pulled in.

Zak slid into the seat beside him. "You okay?"

Donovan flexed his fist. His knuckles were split and bruised. "I think so."

Zak nudged his shoulder. "Bet that felt good, didn't it? I've wanted to punch Mark fucking Salas since high school."

The knot in his gut uncoiled, and the tension he'd carried for fifteen years left him with a small laugh. "We all wanted to punch Mark in high school."

"And you finally got to do it." Zak made a fist and punched his palm. "Now I'm gonna punch him in court. He's going to pay for all the distress he caused my wife and kids."

"Ooh," Cal said as he slid into the front seat. "That sounds fun. Can I help with that?"

"Of course." Zak grabbed his wallet and pulled out a dollar bill, which he passed to Cal. "Here's your retainer. You're officially Redwood Coast Rescue's lawyer."

Cal opened his mouth but closed it again without saying a word and leaned back with a groan. "Aw, fuck. What have I gotten myself into?" But he pocketed the money as Ash jumped into the car and cranked the engine. "Whoa, Sheriff. Where's the fire?"

Ash stared at him for a beat, then pointed to the horizon where flames danced. "The wind's shifted."

chapter
twenty-five

THE FIRE WAS HEADED DIRECTLY toward town.

They had to evacuate.

Now.

Despite Ash's protests, Donovan jumped into his Jeep the moment they reached the sheriff's office and burned rubber home. He'd lost everything else good in his life. His mom. Sasha. He was not leaving his dog behind and losing her, too.

He left the Jeep running in his driveway and sprinted toward his house. It didn't register that his door was open or that Spirit was barking from somewhere deeper in the house, along with another dog. All he saw was Sasha standing in the living room, her eyes brimming with tears.

"Angel, what are you doing here? We're under evacuation orders." He crossed to her in several quick strides, but she flinched back when he reached for her.

And then he saw it.

The vest half-hidden under her coat, strapped over her scrubs. The cylinders, the wires.

"Donovan," she whispered, voice quivering. "He's here somewhere."

He dropped to his knees in front of her and carefully

pushed her coat aside to get a closer look at the bomb vest. "Tiago?"

She nodded. "He called my answering service and said a dog had been found badly burned on the side of the road. I-I grabbed Matilda because I didn't want to leave her alone and went to work and—and he was waiting."

"Did he hurt the dogs?"

She gave a jerky shake of the head. "He shut them in the garage." Tears spilled from her eyes. "I don't know where he went, but he didn't leave. He put this thing on me and said— he said he wants to watch you lose everything."

"Okay, angel. It's okay. Can you lift your jacket and turn for me? Let me see the back of the vest."

She sucked in a shaking breath, but lifted her coat and slowly turned in a circle.

Fuck. It had the same switch as the car bomb, and this time, the bastard had armed all of the fail-safes. Donovan's heart pounded in his ears as he took in the details of the bomb. Tiago had really outdone himself this time. There was no way he could disarm it without setting it off. One wrong move and Sasha would be blown to pieces. He couldn't let that happen.

His bomb kit was still in his car and, with the fire eating its way toward town, he didn't have time to go get it. He stood up and looked around the room, searching for something, anything, that could help him. His eyes landed on his butcher block. His knives weren't as sharp as they should be and had seen better days, but they were all he had handy.

Without thinking twice, he grabbed the entire block off the counter and set it on the floor in front of Sasha.

"Okay, angel," he said, his voice calm and steady. "We're going to get this thing off you. But I need you to trust me."

Sasha nodded, her eyes never leaving his. He could see the fear in them, but he could also see the trust and love she had for him. It gave him the strength he needed.

"Okay, now listen to me very carefully," he said. "I need you to stay perfectly still. Don't move a muscle. I'm going to try and cut the wires on the vest, but I have to be very careful. If I cut them in the wrong order, it could trigger the bomb."

Sasha nodded again, biting her lip so hard that it started to bleed.

He reached down and chose a medium-sized knife from the block, testing the edge with his thumb. Not sharp enough but all he had. He studied the vest, trying to make sense of the tangle of wires and cylinders, then took a deep breath and began to cut. The first wire snapped under the blade, and something on the vest beeped.

"Donovan?" Sasha's voice was barely a whisper.

"I'm here, angel," he said, his voice steady. "It's okay."

He cut the second wire and then the third, his fingers steady despite the thunderous pulse of his heart.

Another wire, and the beeping increased in frequency.

"Donovan," Sasha said, her voice trembling. "Please hurry."

"I'm almost done," he said, his own voice shaking now. He cut through two more wires in quick succession, going too fast, getting too sloppy. The knife slipped and there was a sharp hiss followed by a loud pop. He froze for a second, his heart in his throat, but then he saw that the cylinder he had pierced had only been a dummy.

Sasha sobbed. "Oh, God. Donovan, the fire—"

He glanced over his shoulder and saw a wall of flames devouring the woods around his house. It roared like a wild animal. The dogs howled in the garage.

"I need another minute." He was almost there, he could feel it. Just one more wire and—

The front door crashed open, and Tiago stepped inside, a gun in his hand. "Get away from her. You can't disarm it. You clip that last wire, and we're all dead."

Donovan stepped back and raised his hands slowly. "We're all dead if we stay here much longer."

"Good. I'll enjoy watching you burn, but this time, I'll stay until the end and make sure the job's done."

"Tiago, man. Why are you doing this?"

"Because you murdered Chrissy so she wouldn't tell everyone you killed Darcy, and nobody in this fucking town cares! She was just a drug addict. Another sad overdose. Nobody was doing anything about it, so I took matters into my own hands."

"I didn't kill Darcy. Mark Salas did. He was just arrested for it. And I didn't kill Chrissy, but you're right— someone did, and I'm working with Ash to figure out who." Donovan risked a glance at Sasha. "Let her go, Tiago. This isn't going to solve anything. Chrissy wouldn't want this. She liked Sasha."

Tiago shook his head, his finger tightening on the trigger. "You took everything from me. Now it's your turn."

A crash sounded from the back of the house, and Tiago swung toward it for a split second, but it was enough of a distraction for Donovan to make his move. He hit Tiago at the same time as a furry, dog-shaped bullet. The three of them slammed into the floor, and Spirit sank her teeth into Tiago's arm. He released the gun with a scream. Donovan rolled away and came face-to-face with a stack of explosives.

Fuck.

Tiago had rigged the entire house.

And the fire was getting closer.

"Don't move!" Donovan yelled at Sasha, who had been knocked to the ground during the scuffle. "The whole house is a bomb!"

Tiago scrambled toward the gun and Donovan knew he had only seconds to act.

He grabbed a knife from the block on the floor and lunged at Tiago, plunging the blade into his chest. There was resistance and he leaned into it, then a pop as the knife broke through. Tiago gasped and fell back, his eyes widening in shock as he clawed at the knife sticking out of his chest. His movements slowed, then his hands dropped to his sides, and he exhaled one final time before his eyes glazed over with death.

Donovan stared down at him in disbelief. He had just killed a man.

Again.

But there was no time to dwell on it. The nightmares would have to come later.

He turned to Sasha as fire crawled up his living room wall and grabbed her hand, pulling her to her feet. "We have to go. Now!"

"The vest!"

He swore and grabbed another knife. He wasn't careful as he sawed through the straps holding it on her because—hell, they were as good as dead anyway if they didn't get it off before racing through the inferno bearing down on them. The vest fell to the floor with a thunk, and Sasha jumped away from it.

"Matilda!" She spun toward the garage at the back of the house.

Since the fire was coming from the front, he decided it was as good a direction as any. "Spirit! Let's go!"

The door between the kitchen and garage hung off its hinges. Later, he'd be impressed that Spirit had managed to break through, but now he just jumped over the wreckage and followed Sasha into the garage.

She had Matilda up on her back, the big dog's front paws wrapped tightly around her shoulders. "Where do we go?"

He spotted his bike and then looked at the back door that led out to his patio and beyond that, a cliff dropping into the

Razorrock River. He opened the door, then climbed onto the bike and offered her his helmet.

She followed his gaze and horror bloomed across her features. "Donovan. No."

The ground shook as the first explosion of what promised to be a firework show ripped through the house.

"Fuck," Sasha said on a sob and jumped on the back of his bike, pulling on the helmet.

He grabbed Spirit and hoisted her up in front of him, then revved the engine. "I'm so sorry, Sasha. Hang on to me if you can."

"Just go!"

They careened through the back doorway and raced along the narrow path between the house and the cliff. They made it halfway down the path when a massive explosion shook the ground beneath them, and his house splintered, raining down as deadly shrapnel.

The path gave way beneath the tires.

Sasha shrieked and wrapped her arms around Donovan's waist, hoping that Matilda's claws digging into her shoulders would keep the dog on her back as the superheated air whistled past her ears.

They were going to die.

Another jolt shook her as the bike hit a ledge on the side of the cliff, somehow still upright. They bounced like a ball from one rocky ledge to the next before suddenly plunging into the icy river.

Sasha gasped and sucked in a lungful of water. She swam to the surface, gagging as Matilda's claws dug deeper into her shoulders. Somehow the dog was still clinging to her back like a huge fuzzy book bag.

The poor girl was going to need a lifetime of doggie therapy after this.

She coughed and searched for Donovan. She didn't see him, but Spirit was there, her little black head bobbing in the water next to the crashed bike, paws paddling frantically.

Sasha went under again. When she surfaced, she ripped off the helmet that kept weighing her down. "Donovan!"

He popped up downstream and coughed hard, spitting up water. His head was bleeding, and his eyes looked dazed, but he was in one piece. She swam over to him.

"Get to shore." His voice was strangled as he pointed to the far shore, opposite the fire. "Over there."

They half-swam, half-bobbed across the river, then crawled up the steep, muddy shoreline and collapsed in the mud. On the ridge overhead, the fire snapped and growled, as if angry they had escaped. Smoke clogged the air, and the sky had deepened to an apocalyptic red.

Sasha extracted Matilda from her back. She was bleeding where the dog's claws had dug into her shoulders, but she didn't care.

They were alive.

They were relatively safe down here in the canyon with the cold water feet away.

She took a moment to breathe and hug her dog, then crawled over to Donovan.

His eyes were closed, and blood poured from a gash in his temple. He groaned softly as Spirit worriedly licked at his face.

"Oh, God. Your head. You should've worn the helmet, not me!" Sasha probed around the wound. It looked like he'd been hit by a piece of his house when it exploded. "Are you okay?"

He winced. "Should be... asking you... that."

"I'm not the one bleeding."

He opened one eye to squint at her.

She shrugged. "Much."

"Sasha," he said suddenly, his voice cracking.

She clutched his hand. "Yes, I'm here."

"I did it. I'm sorry."

"What are you talking about?"

"I killed."

"Yes. You did. Well done." She cringed. That didn't come out right. "I mean, you had to do it. You were defending us. You did what you had to do."

"Not him."

She stared at him for a stunned moment. "You didn't kill Darcy. Or Chrissy. I know you didn't."

"No." He held her gaze, his eyes filled with pain. His pupils were different sizes, which was not a promising sign. "My dad."

"Oh." But she wasn't surprised, was she? She'd known it when he told her the story of his family over dinner. And the podcast had only confirmed her suspicions. "The blood on your bat and in your carpet. You were protecting your mom, weren't you?"

He nodded but winced and raised a hand to his temple. "He was going to kill her."

"You did what you had to do then, too. Nobody in the world would hold you accountable for protecting your mom."

"I love you," he whispered, and his eyes rolled back, and his limbs started to jerk.

Oh, God. He was having a seizure. She tried to protect his head from slamming against the rocky shore as best as she could until it passed. When he finally went still, there was little color left in his complexion.

"Donovan. Oh, no. Please." She cradled him and kissed his cheeks, his nose, his lips. "No. Please. I love you, too. Please, come back!"

chapter
twenty-six

Three Months Later

DONOVAN SHUFFLED through the front doors of the ballroom and instantly spotted his angel across the dance floor, shimmering in a pale silver gown as she laughed with his team. Everyone was there—Zak and Anna, Bella and Poppy, Sawyer and Zelda, Pierce, Ash, Cal, and even Veronica, though she looked like she wanted to bolt.

But Donovan only had eyes for one person. It had been a month since he was released from the hospital, and his doctor had given him tentative permission for sex. And he planned to make the most of tonight.

It was New Year's Eve, but this ball was more than a celebration to welcome in the next year. It was marking the start of a new era for Redwood Coast Rescue and the entire town of Steam Valley. It was a celebration of survival and renewal.

Donovan crossed the room in measured strides, his cane tapping the floor like a drumbeat. His balance was shit since the surgery to relieve the pressure in his cracked skull, but he took comfort in knowing that Spirit had bounced back from balance issues after her brain surgery. He could do it, too.

When he reached Sasha, he held out a hand. "Angel, may I have this dance?"

Sasha's smile was as bright as the chandelier overhead. "And speak of the devil," she said over her shoulder to Zak and Anna. "Here's mine come to tempt me away."

He growled low in his throat, pulled her in tight against him, and fastened his lips to hers.

"Oh, get a room, you too," Anna said playfully.

Donovan glanced over his woman's shoulder at their group of friends, then focused in on Sasha's mouth again. "Okay." He grabbed her hand, and she laughed as he pulled her toward the door.

"Hey, Van!" Ash called after him. "Don't forget the other thing we have to do tonight."

"Yeah, give me a couple hours," he called back.

Zak snorted. "That's optimistic, pal. You've been in the hospital for months. It'll only take a couple minutes."

Donovan flipped him the bird.

Sasha giggled all the way up to the room—the same room, she noticed, as their first night together. Her devil never missed a single detail.

As soon as they stepped inside, Donovan dropped his cane and pulled her body flush against his, running his hands along her curves. His fingertips sent a shiver up her spine as he lowered his lips to hers again, exploring her mouth with an urgent need. The heat of his body seemed to envelop her, and she could feel the intensity of his desire, like an electric current running through them both. He cupped her face with both hands and nibbled lightly on her chin, then her neck as his expert fingers worked the laces on the back of her gown.

He wanted her, and he wanted her now.

And, God knew, she wanted him.

But she hesitated and pushed gently against his chest until he pulled back. These past few months had been a terrifying touch-and-go as the doctors worked to mitigate the damage he'd done to his head. "Are you sure this is okay?"

"More than okay." His eyes crinkled in amusement, and he kissed the tip of her nose as he slid one side of her dress off her shoulder. "I had an appointment this afternoon and got the all-clear for sex. That's why I was late getting here."

He slid the other strap off her shoulder, and the dress fell to her waist, her breasts spilling out. He cupped one in his hand, plumping the nipple with the rasp of his thumb. With a male sound of appreciation, he leaned down and licked it, then sucked it into his mouth. The hot suction shot sparks of pleasure directly to her core, and she had to bite her lip in order to keep from moaning out loud.

She had never felt like this with anyone before. His every touch lit her body on fire, and she couldn't wait to spend the rest of her life burning for him. She ran her hand through his hair, feeling the scar of his surgery under her fingers.

God, she almost lost him.

If not for a smokejumper noticing them by the river and calling in a rescue team, she would have. What she thought was just a shrapnel wound had, in fact, been a fractured skull. He'd come close to dying several times that first night. As the fire raged through town, she sat beside him in the ICU of a Sacramento hospital, holding his hand and urging him to fight. The first time his blood pressure crashed, she realized she was an idiot for pushing him away. The second time, she promised she'd never push him away again if he'd just live through the night.

Now, three months later, she had every intention of keeping that promise. She pulled him closer to her chest, moaning softly, encouraging him to suck harder. His possessive grasp tightened on her hips, and he backed her toward the bed, laying her down.

"Do you want my mouth, angel?" As he spoke, his lips moved lower, trailing blazing kisses down her stomach. "Or my fingers?" His hands followed his mouth, caressing her thighs, and then stripping off her thong.

She gasped as he nudged her legs apart with his shoulders and dragged his tongue along her slit. Her core ached, and her entire body tensed as the orgasm built to a peak.

Donovan alternated using his tongue and his fingers, teasing her and making her want more but pulling back just as she trembled at the precipice. She moaned, desperate for him to fill her. Fingers, tongue, cock—she didn't care as long as he stroked the ache inside her. She wrapped her arms around his head, holding him closer. His low chuckle zinged pleasure straight up through her core, and she bucked against his tongue.

Suddenly, he surged up over her, propping himself on his arms as he stared into her eyes. "No, I know what you really want. My cock inside you, pumping until you scream."

Anticipation made her tremble. "Yes."

"My naughty angel." His fingers tangled in her hair, tugging ever so slightly as he leaned in to capture her lips. His kiss devoured her, his tongue exploring with a hunger that had her gasping. She could taste herself on his lips, and it was exhilarating.

Donovan growled low in his throat and broke the kiss, taking his cock in hand. He teased the flared head through her wetness before sinking into her, pressing her into the bed, taking possession of every inch of her skin.

He moved with a slow, steady rhythm, his hands still tangled in her hair as he stared into her eyes. His gaze was so intense, so possessive, and she loved it. The air seemed to stand still between them when they were this close, and she could feel with every cell of her body how much he wanted her.

How much he loved her.

Her back arched, and her legs quivered as the tension built inside her. His hips moved faster, driving her closer to the edge, and a moan escaped her lips as the sensations reached their peak. She hung there, suspended for an endless moment, then the cascade of pleasure took her over.

When she came back, she found him still pumping into her, his movements growing more ragged with each thrust. He tucked his arms under her and pulled her tight against him as if he couldn't get close enough. His body trembled before finally, with one last thrust, he groaned and released, burying his face in her hair.

Outside, the sun made its lazy descent toward the horizon. No longer blood red, it painted the sky in different shades of magenta and cast soft orange light through the window to spill over their bed. Donovan's skin glowed against hers, his natural tan contrasting sharply with her pale complexion.

No other man had ever possessed her heart, body, and soul as he did.

He still clutched her tightly against him, but he'd shifted to his back so as not to crush her, pulling her on top. His fingertips grazed her shoulder, setting off new little sparks along all of her nerve endings. His heart thumped loudly under her ear, and she smiled as she nuzzled in closer to him and inhaled deeply. He smelled of cedar and rain—such an improvement from hospital antiseptic—and she swore she got a buzz just from breathing him in.

"You're mine," he whispered, his voice soft yet firm.

She let out a deep sigh as she melted into his arms. "Yes."

"I love you, Sasha."

Love, shockingly bright and all-encompassing, filled her chest and spread warmth throughout her entire body. They had both lost their homes in the fire, but it didn't matter. His presence was the only thing she needed. Wherever he was had become the place she belonged in the world.

And they'd rebuild something better.

Together.

"I love you, too," she replied, her voice barely a whisper. No hesitation. No worries that she was making a mistake. Donovan Scott may not have been anywhere in her original life plan... but now she couldn't imagine a life without him in it. And she was willing to risk it all to stay with him. "Let's get married."

She felt his lips curve into a smile by her temple. "So marrying the town bad boy is on your checklist now? You want me in a tux for a big June wedding?"

She straddled him and ran her hands up over his tattooed chest. "Fuck the list."

He laughed, the sound booming through the room. "I'd rather fuck you."

She jumped off the bed, shying out of his reach. "You can do that again right after we fly to Vegas tonight and get married by Elvis."

Rolling, he propped himself up on his elbow and watched her pull her dress back on. "Elvis, huh?"

"Or whoever. And wherever. I don't want to wait. I'm done playing it safe."

"That sounds perfect." He slid off the bed and kissed her shoulder before helping her re-lace the dress. "Book the flights." When he turned her to face him, his smile faded. "There's just one thing I have to do first."

"Meet Ash?"

"Yeah."

"I know. Go get it over with and come back to me." She

hated the sudden sadness in his eyes and cupped his cheek, offering a smile. "I'll be at the airport waiting to whisk you off to Vegas and make an honest man out of you."

His grin returned. "Oh, angel. You got your work cut out for you."

epilogue

FROM THE FRONT seat of Ash's Tahoe, Donovan stared at the row of brightly painted Victorian homes on a quiet street in San Francisco.

The robin's egg blue one in the middle was their target.

He rubbed at the back of his neck as tension clamped around his spine. "You're sure she's in there?"

"Positive," Ash said. "She and her husband bought it when his company moved here from New York last summer. You ready for this?"

"No, Goddammit." But he shoved out of the car and strode across the street, his cane too loud on the payment, each tap echoing like a gong inside his barely-healed skull. He'd pushed himself too hard tonight, but he didn't regret it. He'd missed months with Sasha as he recovered from his injuries. He couldn't wait to get this over with so he could return to her.

But he hesitated at the door. Did he really want to know...?

Yes. Fuck it. He deserved to know.

He lifted a hand to knock.

When the woman answered, all the air left his lungs. It was

like getting bitch-slapped with the past. She had haunted him in nightmares and hallucinations for years, and now here she was in the flesh. She looked the same, but also so very different —older and more polished, her hair now blond and her belly heavy with pregnancy. But she had the same eyes, the same sad smile.

"Darcy."

She froze at the sight of him and lifted her face toward the ceiling as if in prayer. But the Darcy he knew had never been the praying type before.

Finally, she stepped back and waved him inside. "Hi, Van."

His lungs wouldn't expand, and all he could manage was one strangled question. "Why?"

Tears flooded her eyes. "I just wanted to disappear and become someone else." She held out her arms and motioned to the clean and bright living room. A diamond bracelet sparkled on her wrist, matching the massive rock on her ring finger. "I'm Mrs. Stella Barclay now, a socialite and CEO's wife, and I'm expecting a baby with the man I love."

"So, you got everything you ever wanted." He shook his head. "And Chrissy's dead now because she helped you escape."

She dropped her arms. "Chrissy's dead because she was a heroin addict."

"Yeah, she was an addict, but she was also clean and sober."

"So was my mom," she spat, and there was the old bitter Darcy he remembered peeking out from under her polish. "For a while, every few months, she'd get clean, but then fucking Frank would hit her again and—" Her gaze shifted away from his as those tears spilled over. She slapped at them in annoyance. "We both know it only takes one time. One slip up."

"No, not Chrissy. She was strong and determined. She was

working the program. Before she died, she told a friend that the military had to be held accountable for her sexual assault. She said it happened to far too many women, and she wasn't just standing up for herself—she was standing up for her best friend, too. When I heard that, I assumed she meant a military friend, but it was *you*. Because of what Mark and JT did to you."

Darcy flinched.

"What really happened to her, Darce?"

She exhaled a long, slow breath and sat down on the snow-white couch stretching in an L across the living room. She didn't speak right away. Just stared off into space and rubbed a hand back and forth over her round belly. "She just had to stay quiet about me. That was all I wanted, but then that fucking podcast came out and started pointing the finger at you again, and Chrissy said she was going to come clean. I told her it was no big deal. It would blow over like it always did—"

"No big deal?" He took a step forward, hands bunched into fists at his side, but stopped himself from touching her. That wasn't why he was here. "I've lived with this hanging over my head for fifteen years, Darcy. I've woken up every morning since you disappeared, wondering if this would finally be the day I was arrested. I've lost friends, missed out on job opportunities, and the entire country thinks I got away with murder. My mom died thinking I was a killer. She never said anything, but I saw how she looked at me when she didn't think I'd notice. Like she was afraid of me. Like I was my father's son, after all. But, yeah, it's no big deal that you're alive. Fuck you."

She burst to her feet, moving faster than a pregnant woman should be able to. "I couldn't come back. You, of all people, know that town was hell for me. And after Mark and JT attacked me—I wanted you all to hurt as much as they hurt me."

"Including Chrissy?"

"No! Chrissy was kind. Probably because she didn't grow up in that cesspool like the rest of us. She found me beaten and brutalized and left to die, and she could've kept walking because she didn't know me. She'd only been at our school for a few months. But she stopped and helped. She wanted to call the police and take me to the hospital, but I begged her not to. If I accused two of the town's golden boys—one of them, the sheriff's son—of rape and attempted murder, nobody would've believed me. So, Chrissy took me to her house."

"And her parents didn't notice?"

She lifted a shoulder. "She was like us. Her parents were never around and didn't care what she was up to. They never knew I was there."

"What about her brother, Tiago?"

"I never saw him. I don't think he ever knew. I only stayed with her for a week until I was strong enough to leave. She stole money from her mom for me, and I made her promise she'd never tell anyone where I'd gone, then I got on a bus to LA and never looked back." Her features twisted in disgust. "Until that podcast. And your therapy group and Chrissy's twelve fucking steps. She thought we wronged you and wanted to make amends."

"And you didn't want to."

"If the truth came out, I'd lose everything. My husband..." She looked down at her belly. "He doesn't know where I came from. He's the best thing that has ever happened to me, and I couldn't risk losing him." She stopped and drew a deep breath. "Last year, when he was in Japan on a business trip, I went back to Steam Valley to talk some sense into Chrissy. She wouldn't listen, so I had to keep her quiet."

"By sticking a fucking needle of fentanyl in her arm?"

She bent double over her belly. "I didn't know it was tainted. I just remembered how my mom was, how she'd forget everything and only cared about her next high, and thought if I got Chrissy addicted again, she'd forget. I didn't mean to kill her, Van."

Donovan closed his eyes and rubbed his chest because it felt like his heart was cracking in half. Part of him, the damaged boy he'd once been, still loved the damaged girl she'd been. "God, Darcy. She was your friend."

"Oh, don't give me that holier-than-thou bullshit. You'd have done the same in my position because we're the same brand of fucked-up."

He opened his eyes and studied her—and, yeah, there was the ugly. It had always been in her. She could dress it up and polish it, but she'd never shed it. It had been one of the things that had attracted him to her in the first place because he'd always thought it was in him, too. How could it not be, given their similar backgrounds?

But Sasha had shown him that wasn't true. She'd seen good in him from the beginning, but he was only now starting to realize she was right. Yeah, he'd come from trash, but he'd never sacrifice an innocent life to save himself and move up in the world. Yeah, he was damaged, but Sasha loved him anyway.

And she was waiting for him so they could start a life together.

But first, he had to finish this.

He walked to the door and opened it. Ash waited on the other side. "Did you hear all that?"

"What?" Darcy said, panic in her eyes as she struggled to get off the couch. "Van! What have you done?"

"Loud and clear," Ash said and stepped inside, his handcuffs already open. "Darcy Cantrell, you're under arrest for the murder of Christina Jimenez."

Donovan watched until the San Francisco PD cruiser disappeared down the street with Darcy inside, then exhaled the air trapped in his lungs.

Ash joined him on the sidewalk. "You doing okay?"

He gave it a second before he answered, checking in with his feelings. He felt... nothing. At least, nothing concerning Darcy. She was still dead to him, he realized, but he was no longer grieving.

He nodded and glanced over at Ash. "Can you take me to the airport?"

Ash cocked an eyebrow. "Why?"

"Sasha's there. We're flying to Vegas tonight and getting married."

Ash stared at him for several heartbeats, then gave a small laugh. "Of course you are. I'd expect nothing less from you."

"It was Sasha's idea."

"Really?" He shook in head in wonder, but said, "Yeah, man, I'll give you a ride. Congrats. She's a good one."

Donovan grinned. "Too good for me?"

"Absolutely." Ash lightly punched his shoulder. "But after all this shit, you deserve some happiness. Now let's go meet your bride."

"Hey, Ash," Donovan called as the guy turned away. "You deserve to be happy, too. Maybe take a vacation, huh? Before you burn out."

Ash just grumbled something under his breath and opened the driver's side door of his Tahoe. "You coming or what?"

Darcy was booked.

Tiago was dead.

Sheriff Jerry had admitted to misleading the investigation to save his son, who had come home that night covered in Darcy's blood.

Mark and JT were flipping on each other and trying to wiggle out of their charges since the woman they allegedly killed was still drawing breath—and actually now booked into the women's wing of the prison they currently called home. But they weren't getting out. They still had to face rape charges and probably attempted murder. The photos Mark had kept all these years were too damning to ignore.

Ash sighed as he dropped into his office chair and wondered how many other cases had been mishandled under Jerry Tennison's watch. He had to investigate everything Jerry touched now—re-examine the closed cases, and take a good, hard look at all the open cold cases.

And he knew exactly where to start.

He created a new folder on his computer and dragged over the picture of the burned bones from the Cantrell case file. He labeled it.

2023- Double R Fire Jane Doe.

When preliminary tests indicated the bones belonged to a female who had once broken her wrist, everyone was sure the DNA would come back matching Darcy—including him. The plate in her wrist and the resulting scar had been a well-documented fact in her file. He'd never even considered the body might be someone else until the DNA test results came back negative for Darcy Cantrell—but, surprise! Darcy's DNA *was* a match for a woman currently living in San Francisco.

What a fucking mess.

"I'm sorry, Jane," he whispered. "I promise I'll find you justice."

He stared at the picture a moment longer. The blackened skull grinned at him.

Then he got back to work.

The Redwood Coast Rescue adventure continues with Ash Rawlings' book, **Searching for Justice.**

And if you'd like to see how it all started, pick up Zak's book, **Searching for Rescue**.

Thanks for reading!

also by tonya burrows

Too Wilde to Tame